MW01137915

The Warmth
of Snow

by Mary Pessaran

Abby Girl
Publishing

I

Title ID: 9099455

Title: ***The Warmth of Snow:***
         A Christmas Story

Description: ***The Warmth of Snow*** is an enchanting seasonal adventure. Sandy Jones and Bill "Mac" McAllister refuse to confine their holiday spirit to one season. With a little help from a fifteen-year-old daughter, an all-knowing grandmother, and a boy with a tuba, they might find their way back to the joy of the Christmas season.

ISBN-13: 978-1727511291
ISBN-10: 1727511298

Primary Category: Fiction
Country of Publication: United States
Language: English
Search Keywords: novel, romance, Christmas
Author: Mary Pessaran

Abby Girl Publishing, 134 Gilded Rock Way
Folsom, California 95630 USA

First Edition, September 27, 2018

Dedication

This story is dedicated to my great-nephew, Owen Jack Broxterman, whose short life touched so many. Owen continues to remind us that every moment matters and the love you share with others is never forgotten.

The Warmth of Snow

IV

Spring

The Warmth of Snow

Chapter One

Sandy

Sandy Jones stepped back to view her latest purchase—a Santa with sunglasses and a bearded grin perched atop a surfboard. She angled the statuette closer to the photo of her father—also sharing the spotlight with a surfboard—and wondered if he might now resemble this roly-poly fellow; thirty years could change a man. Perhaps the tribute was too obvious. She removed the sun-loving St. Nick from the mantel and set him next to the ornament tree currently covered in shamrocks. She smiled at the unintentional festive combination of green and red.

"You do know it's March, right?" The dissenting voice was that of her mother, Candace, whom she never referred to as "Mother" or "Mom" or any name that might indicate a status beyond free spirit. The "free spirit" had dropped by announced—again.

"This Santa just arrived last week," Sandy defended. "He needs to adjust to his new home before I pack him away."

"He's wearing swim trunks. I think he's never going to adjust to March in St. Clair, Indiana. It snowed last week."

She had a point, but was it Sandy's fault they'd moved away from California before she had even celebrated her first birthday? If they'd still been living in Huntington Beach where she was born, snow would not have entered either of their minds. Candace granted the Santa one more glance before holding her hand up to examine her nails. "At least there's only *one* of them."

Sandy wasn't going to remind her about the other Kris Kringles who kept her company throughout the year. On the buffet in the dining room, a bespectacled fellow sat calmly in his sleigh reading the Nice List. Upstairs in the guest room, a Santa with an overflowing bag of toys promised gifts. In the bathroom, a small, unassuming carved glittery gent had found a spot on a shelf while a helpful fabric Santa holding onto a string of socks resided in the laundry room. The rest of Sandy's collection had begrudgingly gone into storage in boxes in the attic. She assumed they all agreed with her that confining Christmas to a very short month was unfair, but her mother would not share any of their opinions.

Candace plopped onto the couch, setting down the can of Sprite she'd grabbed out of Sandy's refrigerator, ignoring the "a coaster for every drink" house rule.

Sandy grabbed a ceramic coaster from the stack on the table, hoping to slip it underneath the can before Candace could see the smiling Santa face painted happily on the coaster.

Candace squinted in disapproval, accenting her new eyelash extensions, as the friendly face went under the rule-breaking can. "Feel better?" she asked.

Sandy would feel better when her mother revealed the purpose of her visit. Candace was a woman of purpose. "You never said why you're here," she prompted.

"*We're* going out." Candace pulled a file from purse and began a slow manicure. "The Beer Dogs are playing tonight at The Rusty Nail."

Sandy noted her mother's attire. With a short jean skirt, matching vest, red cowboy boots and recently dyed blonde hair, she was party-ready. "You're going to The Rusty Nail? You work there nearly every night. Why not try someplace new?"

Candace glared over the top of her hand. "*You're* suggesting someplace new?"

"I'm only saying…" What was she saying? Candace didn't need her advice on how to have fun. "Never mind. I'm happy for you and whoever is in your pocket, but I'm staying in."

Candace made a mock showing of looking in her vest pocket. "Kevin will be there, and he's bringing a friend."

Rather than remind her for the hundredth time that she *hated* country music and that she already *had* a boyfriend, Sandy simply said, "Trent's coming over."

"What? It's Thursday. I thought Tuesday was your night." She said it as if it were a rule that couldn't be broken, which before tonight may have been true.

"Well, he's coming over *tonight* so you need to scoot. You can call me tomorrow and tell me about the winner of a guy Kevin had planned for me." A few years ago, Sandy had given in to her mother's insistence that she needed to get out more, and had regretted it all night. Her surprise date had more hands than the collection of clocks in her grandmother's living room, or so it seemed on the dance floor. "By the way," Sandy said to end the conversation, "I liked you better as a redhead."

Candace laughed. She tucked the nail file back into her purse and pushed herself off the sofa. "And I think you need to live a little. I haven't been blonde in years, and it was time for a change. Besides, Kevin likes blondes."

Yes, Kevin liked blondes, and redheads, and brunettes, but Sandy saw no reason to remind Candace of that fact. If her mother were true to her history with men, she would be done with Kevin long before he was ready to move onto the next hair color. Sandy scooped up Candace's coat from the back of couch and held it out to her.

Candace folded her arms like a rebellious child. "What's the big occasion anyway?"

Sandy wished she had more practice in the fine art of bluffing, or lying if the situation called for it. "Tonight is special. That's all I have to say."

"Don't tell me he's going to *propose*." Candace spit out the word as if Trent were plotting to kidnap her.

"If Trent were going to propose, I'd have purchased a new outfit." As it was, she was still wearing her light pink cashmere sweater and black pencil skirt from her day at work as the manager of Ginger's, an upscale women's clothing store. If she could convince Candace to leave, she could hurry upstairs and slip into the sleek muted ebony dress that Trent once said he liked. He gave out compliments like Scrooge giving out Christmas bonuses, so she held onto each one. "I'll let you know when you need to start shopping for a lace mother-of-the-bride dress, unless you plan on wearing that—"she motioned to Candace's jean skirt—"to my wedding."

"Oh, I'll wear the lace, but the cowboy boots stay. Is he moving in?"

"No, he's not moving in. We're just having dinner. Takeout, if you must know." She knew it sounded pathetic. They had never been the most exciting of couples. During the two years they'd been together, they'd developed a routine: Sunday brunch at Rico's, Tuesday night dinner at her house, Friday night at his apartment, and they *never* did takeout. Trent preferred the healthier—and less expensive—option of cooking at home.

Lately, however, Sandy found herself feeling restless, somehow wearied by the unwavering rituals that she initially found comforting but now seemed tedious.

Tonight, they were taking a big step toward breaking their patterns, the change in routine a result of her subtle, but persistent, suggestions they were getting old before their time. Trent was on the cusp of thirty, a milestone she'd passed last year. He'd said she was using the decade marker against him to her advantage, but agreed to pick up dinner anyway. The event might not warrant a new outfit, but Sandy believed in the power of the "right dress" to nudge Trent toward her point of view.

"Takeout?" Candace said with a slight question but also understanding.

"Takeout." Sandy opened the door to discourage any further discussion.

Candace accepted her coat and flung it across her shoulders. "Well, you know where we'll be." Her eyes softened. "You could bring the boy along. I figure if you can manage takeout on Thursday, surely you can handle the Texas Two-Step." Leaving Sandy with the visual of Trent's gangly legs shuffling around the dance floor, Candace and her boots walked out the door.

Sandy sometimes envied her mother's confidence but not her dating record. She'd only made spotty references to Sandy's father, but Sandy believed Candace had spent her whole life pining over the surfer who'd stolen her heart in a flash and left her as quickly. She seemed to discount every other suitor who never had a chance of taking his place. She wanted a better outcome for her daughter. Sandy thought Trent *was* a better outcome. He might never master country line dancing, but he was steady, and he was *there*, not off somewhere searching for the perfect wave.

As Candace sped away, Sandy's cell phone rang. Seeing Trent's name, her heart quickened. As silly as it sounded, all day she'd imagined the delights that Trent might bring—mu shu pork from Bo Lings, fajitas from Jose's, or curry from the new Indian buffet on Sixth. A new restaurant—a new beginning.

"Hi, Trent," she answered. "Are you on your way?"

"Hey, Sandy. How's it going?"

His too-casual greeting said he wasn't on his way. Her excitement faded. "I'm fine. Where are you?"

"Yeah, so here's the thing. You know Reynaldo got promoted."

She knew very well about Reynaldo's promotion. Trent felt slighted, and for a couple of weeks after the announcement, she'd heard the low grumble of discontent. Sandy thought Reynaldo's seniority warranted the upward movement, but she chose not to share that thought with Trent. Recently, he had seemed more relaxed, even with the overtime required to train Reynaldo's replacement. She couldn't say what had caused the change in disposition, but she was grateful for a happier boyfriend.

"I can't get away right now." Sandy thought his tone should be more apologetic. "I'll see you tomorrow night, right?"

She'd pushed him and he'd pushed back in a way that would make protests from her sound petty and unreasonable. She couldn't argue with a work excuse, but she could mentally stamp her feet and cry, *Not fair.* "Sure, Trent. I'll see you tomorrow night. Same as always." She didn't mask the disappointment in her voice.

"Okay," he said too cheerfully, "I'll see you then."

"Trent," she said, catching him before he clicked off, "what were you going to bring for dinner?"

8

"For dinner?" He'd likely spent as much thinking about it as he did choosing his wardrobe. She assumed he was wearing his favorite argyle sweater, the same one he would have been content to wear every day. "Pasta, maybe."

"What kind of pasta?"

"I'm not sure. The blackened-chicken pasta from Rico's? It's your favorite, right?"

The dish was a favorite, one she ate nearly every week. He had completely missed the point of the evening, or maybe not showing up was his way of saying that the need for change in their relationship was Sandy's alone. "Yes, it's one of my favorites."

He paused. She suspected he was calculating his next response, as if she were one of his computer coding problems. "We can have pasta tomorrow night, if you want."

"No. It's fine. Let's just stick to the plan."

"Sounds good." He took the opportunity to hang up.

She held the now silent phone in her hand and stood at her picture window. The maple tree in her front yard just last week had popped with buds. Spring brought the promise of new life, but her old life seemed determined to hold her in place.

She didn't need a new dining experience. She didn't need Trent to propose or to move in, or even to lead her around a dance floor. She certainly didn't need the kind of love her mother had for Sandy's father, the kind that broke her heart every day. She simply wanted a little spark—something that said tomorrow might be different from today.

She wiped away a tear. She'd never been good at lying, not even to herself. She wanted more than a spark. She wanted the fire. Even if it broke her heart.

Chapter Two

Bill

Bill McAllister had sequestered himself in his garage workshop, rigging a mechanical arm on a wooden snowman. He had engineered the innocent-looking snowman to throw tennis balls, painted white, at a cutout of a naughty boy holding the snowman's carrot nose. In theory, the "snowballs" should hit their target, fall into the bin below, roll back to snowman's gloved hand and wait in line for the next throw. In reality, they were bouncing off the board, landing on the concrete and rolling under cabinets and workbenches.

He wanted this piece to be the center of his outdoor Christmas display, but its continued resistance had him reconsidering its place of honor. He rubbed his chin, thinking about a different candidate for the lead position. He envisioned a snowman sliding down the hill on a sled with an electric fan hidden behind a tree to show the scarf blowing in the wind. He'd add it to the list. Right now, the mechanical snowman missing his nose and the petulant child about to be pummeled with snowballs called to him. He went back to work, digging through the bin next to his workbench for the right screwdriver.

The search would have been easier if he would take the time to organize his workshop. They'd moved to St. Clair over two years ago right after Thanksgiving. With the move and his new job as the construction manager for a new home developer, he'd been busy then with less time to build that year's holiday exhibit. He could have skipped the intricate display—none of his new neighbors would have known—but transplanting the snow village to this home felt like a priority that couldn't wait. He'd never regretted putting aside mundane tasks like adding shelves to his garage in favor of setting up his snow comrades, complete with illuminating lights, to greet their visitors. He had planned to texture the garage walls and lay an epoxy floor before adding more storage space. The following spring would have been the optimal time to complete the work. It hadn't happened. Since them, he'd had the time, but not the desire.

He glanced at the pegboard tucked behind a box in the corner. He could mount it on the wall above his workbench and hang the rest of his tools. He'd think about it. Fixing his garage meant this was his life, and right now, he was satisfied with leaving the garage unfinished and his life unsettled.

The door creaked open, and, for the hundredth time, he reminded himself to spray some WD-40 on its hinges. Gwen stood in the doorway with her arms crossed, a stance she took regularly in his environment. "You *do* know it's March, right?" She liked to remind him of the seasons, emphasizing *not Christmas* with each comment. She was wearing a little white leather jacket, and with her short red hair, she mildly resembled a candy cane, but wasn't nearly as friendly.

A month ago, she'd shown up with a new haircut saying, "I've tamed my curls in submission." He missed the chaotic curls whose bounce rose and fell with the weather patterns, but she liked the controlled hairdo. Sometimes he worried he might be next in line to be tamed into submission. "Hey, Gwen," he said, choosing a sweet tone to counteract the tartness in hers. "I didn't hear your car pull up."

"You were concentrating. I thought you would have been done with that snowman by now."

"He's being stubborn. I know I said I wouldn't spend so much time on this project but it gets hot in here in the summer. I'd like to do this now." He stepped toward her, giving her a quick kiss.

She responded by lowering her crossed arms.

He took it as a truce and motioned her to his workbench. "I'd like to get you opinion on something." He laid out the sketch of his display. "I'm thinking of building a small hill, so I can have a snowman sliding down. I could also add a snowman here"—he pointed to a spot on the drawing—"with a shovel, building the hill."

Gwen stared at the plan with intense green eyes that Bill had always liked but now seemed critical. "Seems a little busy." She scrunched her small nose. "Why do you need so many? Aren't they all the same?"

"Well, I guess. I mean they're all snowmen, but..." How could he explain the differences, not just in appearance, but also in personality? The fun-loving sledding snowmen were nothing like the reverent carolers. The impish boy had no worries, unlike the stoic snowman with bendable legs forced to sit on a bench. The daredevil snowman skier had marked determination, while the graceful skaters on the icy pond were completely serene.

People drove for miles to see his exhibits, not just because of the lights, the overhead music, and the cups of special recipe hot chocolate he prepared each year, but because the snow village invited people to come into their Christmas world and celebrate. Last year's display had won him a blue ribbon in the city competition for best use of animation. Gwen said it was "clever" but also asked if it was worth the hours he labored over it and the added electricity costs (which were substantial, but he wouldn't admit it to her). *It's worth it*, he had wanted to scream but she had planted questions that had stayed with him, and he was finding it more difficult to defend his hobby.

"I bought a lemon meringue pie," Gwen said, offering her alternative to listening to Bill's plan. "It's in the kitchen. Would you like a piece?"

"Sure," he said, feeling defeated. "Give me another couple of minutes and I'll be in."

She folded her arms again, ending the truce. "You say that every time, Mac," she said, using his nickname, "but it's always longer. I think I might need to cover myself in white spray paint to get some attention from you."

Bill imagined them as a snow couple, with coal for eyes and carrots for noses, smiles frozen on their faces.

"Amanda could use more time with you, too," she added.

Bill wasn't certain he could agree. At fourteen, Amanda had more interesting things to do than hang out with her father. Her school activities and social calendar took most of her evenings, and homework was non-negotiable. Even so, a pang of guilt threaded its way in. "After she gets home from volleyball practice, I'll have some time with her. And you're right. This can wait, too. Now, let's have some of that pie."

Gwen smiled and hurried inside to slice the prized lemon meringue. As Bill reached for the light, he flashed on another idea for his snow village. He took a step toward the plans and stopped. "It's March," he told himself. "There's time." But it didn't feel like there was time. It never felt like there was enough. Every second counted. He was running as fast as he could, but he could never catch up.

He flipped off the light. Outside, he heard a large truck approach, the sound growing louder and then fading as it slowed for the stop sign at the corner. The brakes squeaked.

He stood motionless as a wave of pain passed through him. "Ellen," he whispered into the darkness. The truck shifted into gear and the rumble continued on its way. Bill steadied himself and went inside for a piece of pie.

Chapter Three

Sandy

Sandy lingered in her car as ice formed on her windshield. The rain had turned to sleet, a late winter storm challenging a bid for spring. The days offered glimpses of summer mixed with harsh reminders of winter's tenacity. It was a typical March in Indiana.

She stared at the hand-painted wooden sign of Althea's Christmas Shop where she had purchased her first Santa—a four-foot high red-coated giant she had named "The General." Since that first purchase, Sandy had fallen under the store's magical spell, the lights, tinsel and twinkling stars igniting childhood dreams of the perfect Christmas, all in one convenient, year-round, VISA accepting location.

Althea's had always been a safe haven; Trent called it her therapy. Recently, the description wasn't too far off. Her efforts to shake up their routine had made her "therapy" visits more frequent, causing some damage to her credit card.

During the last holiday season, he had chaffed at the bounty of her Christmas spirit. With all the Santas surrounding her, she felt happier and she wanted to give presents, which, according to Trent, she did *too much*. He went along with her "everyone gets a present" rule when it came to her family, and his, and even her employees, but when it extended as far as the postal carrier, he'd had enough. She could have reminded him of the number of presents "Santa" had left for him under her tree, but she agreed to take a few people off the list (what he didn't know wouldn't hurt him).

She felt responsible for the tension that now hung between them like icicles on the edge of a roof. She was the one who had changed. He was the same Trent she'd met two years earlier at the opening reception of a local artist's exhibit, bonding over wine and appetizers. The relationship had worked, until it hadn't, when she'd started pushing them to stretch beyond the boundaries they had both set for themselves.

Sandy looked out through the now translucent car window, covered in ice. She loved this street during the holiday season. On Thanksgiving night, the town held its tree lighting ceremony, bringing the season to life. Every streetlamp held a lighted wreath with trees lining the median, reminiscent of Bedford Falls in *It's a Wonderful Life*. She could almost see Jimmy Stewart running down the street after he remembered all the reasons he had to live.

Maybe Trent was right. Maybe it all was *too much*.

She started to shift the car out of park, ready to let it go, when she saw *him*. He came out of the hardware store two doors down, pulling his collar around his neck. Her heart responded with a few extra beats.

She'd first noticed *him* on a misty November night a few months ago. She'd stopped by Althea's after a bad day at work, the seasonal inventory overload at Ginger's taking its toll on both her and her employees. She had survived five Christmases at the upscale retail shop and could almost predict the moments when everyone wanted to scream a collective "bah humbug." The frustration never lasted, but she'd needed a break.

That night, as she'd browsed through Althea's deciding which of the new Santa arrivals she would add to her collection, she'd turned to find a set of bright hazel eyes upon her. The man behind them withdrew slightly, acting as though he'd been caught.

"Hard to choose?" he'd asked, averting his eyes toward the nearest shelf.

She'd opened her mouth to respond, but couldn't get past his dark eyebrows, long eyelashes and the smile that played at the corner of his lips. She'd managed a quiet, "Yes."

"I have the same problem." He'd held up two snowman contraptions tucked beneath his arm. "This one sings 'Frosty the Snowman.' How can you not love the classics?" He'd pushed a button on the unfortunate plastic figure. The song burst forward in synthesized melody as the arms moved in a rhythm that was for a different beat entirely. "This one," he'd held up the other, "skates on a pond. No singing, unfortunately, but I think we'll get a little music in the background."

He'd pushed aside a Victorian Santa on the shelf wearing his Christmas best (she was certain if the refined Mr. Klaus could respond, he would have been annoyed), and plunked Frosty down in the space. He'd held the skating snowman and flipped the switch. The little snowman made a circular trip around the mirrored pond. The song from the jubilant Frosty wanted to upstage the velvety tones of "Let it Snow," creating a discordant chorus.

He'd laughed, pulling her in.

"That one." She'd pointed to the skating snowman. "He's quieter."

"Not a Frosty fan?" His words were innocent, but the intensity of his gaze suggested something not nearly so innocent.

She'd felt color on her cheeks, acutely aware of the flutter his proximity created, and even more aware of the ring on his left hand. She should have smiled and politely turned back to her Santas, but she'd wanted to move closer. His eyes seemed to hold her in place. To add to her conflicting emotions, an uninvited comparison with Trent played in her head.

Unlike Trent, this man was not tall, but somehow the perfect height. She'd imagined herself fitting perfectly under his arm. He had wide, strong shoulders that she suspected matched muscular legs under his well-fitted jeans. His thick brown hair framed a face that begged for a "ruggedly handsome" description. Trent had a mop of sandy hair on top of a tall, wiry frame, and a crooked smile on his boyish face. There was nothing boyish about the man in front of her. His face was seasoned, but filled with life. Sandy had to form a fist to keep from reaching out and touching the stubble on his chin. She'd forced one more glance at his hand, foolishly hoping the ring had disappeared.

"Well, then," he'd drawn back after he noticed Sandy's focus on his ring finger, "Frosty will have to find another home. Do you need any help?" He'd pointed to the selection of Santas she had lined up.

She had wanted to say, "Yes," but "No," is what came out, followed by a cursory, "Thank you."

He'd nodded, picked up Frosty and returned to the section that played host to the snow brigade, replanting the figure among similar models. He'd tucked the skating snowman under his arm.

When he'd left the store with *her* choice of snowmen, she quickly dismissed her reaction, assuring herself it was a chance one-time encounter. Then she saw him again in December, in January and then February. She realized she had met a mutual dedicated shopper, even in the off-season, a perilous attribute when paired with strong arms and a charismatic smile. Each time, she'd say, "Hello" or wave and sometimes they'd chat. His enthusiasm for his hobby was also a magnet for other shoppers to join in the fun as he demonstrated his boisterous frosty friends. She loved listening to his infectious laugh.

Sometime around Valentine's Day, she'd started having fantasies about him, the dangerous kind that involved a shared future. She pictured the two of them sitting on her couch on a Sunday morning reading the paper. He would cook her pancakes while she poured Mimosas and they would plan their day. He would reach for her, his insistent hands wrapping around her waist, pulling her toward him. His lips would caress hers. And then . . .

She knew she had to stop—to stop seeing him, to stop fantasizing, to stop wishing for something that could never happen.

Put the car in drive, she told herself. Her hand refused to move. Seeing him again ignited desires from deep within her. Her heart was pounding in a way that was completely unacceptable, but too consuming to ignore.

He stepped toward Althea's and stopped, gazing up at the wooden sign. He wiped the sleet from his face and ducked inside. She turned off her car, grabbed her umbrella and followed him in.

The tinkle of the bell announced her arrival. Althea's was silent, devoid of the usual upbeat music designed to cause a shopping frenzy. A young sales associate stood near a glass shelf, removing Lenox Easter bunny figurines from their bubble-wrap security. "We're closing early," the girl warned. An ice storm that allowed an early closing must be akin to a school snow day.

Sandy set her umbrella by the door, scanning the store for the man she knew would be in his favorite snowman section. Instead of being obvious and marching toward him, she stopped by a shelf of Santas where her latest object of desire waited for her adulation.

This Santa was only ten inches high, but his coat was made of burlap with shorn wool bordering the hood and sleeves. His boots were real leather with tiny leather shoelaces. In her heart, Sandy had already claimed him, the price tag a minor obstacle she would overcome. For now, she was content to pick up the Santa and hold it while she surreptitiously observed the only other shopper in the store.

A mechanical snowman had captured his attention. He flipped a lever and the snowman tipped his hat. The simple gesture should have evoked a laugh, but it almost seemed to aggravate him. He set it on the table, gaping as if the inanimate object might reveal an answer to a difficult question. Then he placed two snowman statues next to one another, scrutinizing them with the same intense concentration. As he did, he twisted his wedding ring, a habit she'd observed before.

The truth of the habit should have pushed her out the door, but seemed to have the opposite effect on her.

She settled the desired Santa back into his temporary home, reassuring him they'd be together soon. When she turned around, hazel eyes were upon her. She took the steps forward and stood in front of him, content to look in those eyes.

"Baffled by the snowmen again, I see." She motioned toward the statues. "Maybe I can help."

He gave the blameless snowmen a reproachful look. "They're all the *same*."

20

"Not really," she encouraged. "The obvious difference is the color of the scarves. Personally, I think red and green are overdone. The red and blue is more subtle, but still festive. You'll notice the carrot nose on this one"—she pointed to the snowman with the red and blue scarf—"is slightly off-center, which makes him more approachable, and his eyes are just a tiny bit friendlier, don't you think?"

He followed her gesture and nodded slowly. "Maybe a tiny bit."

He shifted his gaze, allowing it to flow over and linger on the features of her face. She could almost feel him taking in the strands of her hair and draw his fingers across her cheeks. He smiled when his survey reached her nose and gasped almost inaudibly when it fell to her lips.

In the light, his eyes carried shades of green, exploding with flecks of yellow. They were . . . fireworks.

He shook his head, as if waking himself from a dream. He lowered his gaze to the snowmen, the prior moment's intimacy evaporating in a puff.

Sandy wished he'd ask her to go for coffee. Or cocoa. She loved cocoa. She wanted to sit across from him and look into the fire of his eyes so they could talk. She wanted him to tell her what had taken away the joy of the frosty gang she knew he loved so much. Instead, she joined him in his study of the two statues, similar and yet completely different. He picked up one and then the other, which led her to observing his hands. They were rough and solid, the kind of hands that knew a day's work and held responsibility. They were an honest and faithful man's hands.

The guilt was heavy in her chest now, not simply because he was married, but because the only barrier keeping her from pursuing him was his ring, and not the love she thought she had for Trent.

He picked up both statues, leveled one more glare, and then plunked them on the shelf, the force appearing to surprise him. "Well, I should get home," he said, regrouping into the friendly stranger. "You should get home, too. The streets are getting slick."

Sandy thought if he had a hat, he might have tipped it. She could compare him to a snowman and they could both laugh, except the laughter seemed to have vanished from his eyes. She could only watch as his broad shoulders walked out the door.

With a glance at the burlap-coated Santa who would not be going home with her tonight, she picked up the snowman with the red and blue scarf, tweaked its crooked carrot nose and carried it to the register.

Chapter Four

Amanda

Amanda McAllister had done it again. She'd thrown everything into one load in the washer and forgotten about it. Now she would have to rewash the clothes before they went into the dryer to get rid of that sour smell she hated. She closed the lid and promised herself she'd do laundry tomorrow. She wished she'd remembered to bring home the bag that contained her wadded up school clothes, but she was in a rush after volleyball practice and the bag had stayed in her locker. Now she'd have to pull out an old pair of jeans from the bottom of a drawer. She was never at a loss for sweatshirts, but she was out of socks. Again.

Sometimes she wished she didn't have to think about adult responsibilities like laundry, or whether they had spaghetti sauce in the pantry, or catching a ride home from school on days when her dad couldn't get away from work. Her life was different from the way it had been when they lived in Lafayette, but she liked living in St. Clair. Her school had fewer students and she felt like she counted. She'd made great friends, and her activities kept her busy. She had a good life for a teenager, if she did say so herself. But it certainly wasn't perfect, and there was a gap no one knew how to fill.

Gwen Novak, her dad's girlfriend, had tried to step in, but Amanda had set some boundaries. She could tell Gwen was hurt.

Amanda couldn't help it. She had a hard enough time taking care of her emotions and those of her dad's. He always said he was fine, but he wasn't. He hadn't been fine since the night her mother had died.

When he'd first met Gwen, he had seemed to perk up. They'd all go out for pizza, play board games and laugh the way Amanda remembered. Now he was quiet again and spent too much time in the garage working on his snowmen, which would have been okay except he seemed to be using it as a hiding place. He would pretend everything was normal, but sometimes it made their conversations weird. She thought he'd be getting better by now, but, if it were possible, he might be getting worse.

She couldn't think about it now; she needed to meet Lacey to study geometry. Her math grade was always on the edge, and her grades were one thing she didn't want her dad to worry about. He had enough on his mind.

Amanda went into her dad's bedroom to borrow a pair of socks. She'd been borrowing his socks for years. He kept them in a special drawer, separate from his underwear—thank goodness. He used to leave funny notes attached to the socks. "*Not us, Amanda. Dad needs to wear us to work.*" Or he'd surprise her and buy crazy pink ones. "*Pick us, pick us!*," the socks would say. The socks hadn't talked to her in a couple of years—two years, one month, and fifteen days to be exact. Two years, one month and fifteen days since her mother's car accident, the night that everything changed.

Memories sometimes whirled around her head. Amanda had worn a new pair of socks that day that her dad had left for her to find. The note had said—"*Oh no, Amanda. These are definitely Dad's*"—except they were her size and had crazy colored stripes. She'd worn them under her boots, giggling with her mom on the ride to school, saying she should steal his other socks and leave him only this pair for work.

It was the last time she ever saw her mom—and she was laughing.

Amanda liked that part, but she always wondered why, when her mom dropped her off at school, she'd reached over and hugged her and held her for a few seconds longer than usual. Did she somehow know she wouldn't see her that night? Amanda hoped not.

They'd let school out early due to a winter storm. Her dad had picked her up and taken her to his office. He had worked, while she did her homework. On the way home, they'd stopped at Rico's to pick up dinner. That's when he'd received the call. She wished she could forget the way his whole body seemed to crumple as he listened to the words.

She couldn't think about it now. She had geometry to study.

Amanda grabbed an acceptable black pair of socks from her dad's drawer to go under her jeans. She shook her head at the mess of clothes scattered across his bed. They were clean, but her dad hated putting clothes on hangers. He used to put in more effort at being neat and organized. Now it seemed like he thought it didn't matter. Things still mattered, even without her mom there.

She missed her mom and sometimes envied the relationship her friends had with their mothers, but she still felt like herself. She was the same person she was before her mom died, just a little more alone. Her dad wasn't the dad she remembered. He still made time for her, but sometimes she wished he'd stopped trying so hard. Then she wouldn't feel bad when she wanted to be with her friends.

Which, she remembered, she needed to do right now.

She decided to hang up a few of his shirts before she left. Gwen would do it if he'd let her, but he had also set some limits. She was nice, and helpful, and a great cook, but everything she did seemed to require something in return. But that wasn't Amanda's problem. It was her dad's, and she couldn't help him solve it.

She opened the closet and removed some hangers—there were plenty of empty ones available. She noticed a paper bag by some shoeboxes on the top shelf. The bag had the Althea's Christmas Shop stamp on it. He'd been shopping—again. She wasn't surprised that he was keeping it in his closet. Gwen wasn't a fan of her dad's hobby, but Amanda knew her dad; he'd find a way to carry on.

Amanda peeked inside the bag, curious to see the newest addition to the snow family. The bag contained a box with a picture on the outside of a Santa Claus. She opened the box and pulled out the padding. Inside was a small statue of Santa Claus wearing a burlap coat and leather boots.

"A Santa!" she laughed. "Now I *know* Dad is losing it!"

Chapter Five

Bill

Bill twisted the ring on his left hand, a habit he knew he fallen into, one he needed to stop. If he put away his ring, the habit would take care of itself. Gwen had voiced her opinion on the subject, but sometimes he just needed to put on the ring, to have it ground him again. He wasn't foolish enough to pretend that nothing had changed, that he was still married to his first love. Sometimes he simply needed the weight on his finger to keep him from floating away.

Gwen wasn't Ellen. That was the whole point. Ellen had been tall and thin with blonde hair that she complained was too fine, but Bill liked the simplicity of it. Ellen had an artistic side that she downplayed and a childlike quality that often had her falling into giggles. Gwen was more practical. She was also more nurturing, sometimes too much, but she cared about Bill and Amanda and wanted to expand her role in their lives. Lately, she'd been pushing to move in, making suggestions on changes in décor. She said her overstuffed sofa would be a good replacement for the leather couch that had been with them since he and Ellen got married. He cringed at the thought of floral throw pillows crowding his space, but maybe a dramatic change was what they needed. His couch was looking worn, and he knew it was time to let it go.

27

Let it go. Let *her* go. How many times had he heard the words from well-meaning friends and family? It seemed ridiculous. He had no choice. Ellen was gone. The finality of it left him feeling empty, as if the loss of the glow of Ellen's life had also taken his along with it. The memories of them together were starting to fade. That reality seemed the cruelest of all.

His world came to a halt just over two years ago. A late season storm with freezing rain had lain down a sheet of ice beneath several inches of snow. Ellen had been on her way home from work. Bill had told her to leave early from the office, but she had a project, a deadline to meet. Afterwards, no one could tell him which project had been so damned important.

Ellen had started through a green light, an intersection she had passed every day since they moved to St. Clair. A truck coming from the side hit a patch of ice. Bill could visualize the slide, the driver pressing his brakes with every bit of power within him, unable to stop the action set into motion.

The weeks and months that followed became a blur of faces and kind words. The father of a motherless twelve-year-old girl grieves differently than a husband who has lost his wife. He suppresses his emotion and forces himself to leave his house. He laughs more when others are around. He returns to an empty house and cries silently and alone. When people ask how he and his daughter are doing, he answers, "We're fine, thanks." And when a woman comes along who wants to take care of him, to fill the expanse of his bed, that man grabs the life preserver she's offering.

Now, he didn't know if a life preserver was enough. He didn't know if he even wanted to try anymore. All he wanted to do was to take a walk with his wife, the mother of his child. He wanted to hike through the woods on the trail they used to love, hold her hand and talk, or simply be quiet, listening to the sounds of the forest. He wanted to sit on the couch beside her—their old couch—and tell her about his day. He wanted to listen as she bragged about another amazing feat of their beautiful daughter.

But Ellen wasn't here, and she would never be here again. Gwen was here now, and despite their differences, she was offering him a chance to pull out of the darkness that seemed to be defeating all of his previous methods for battling it.

Last year, his doctor prescribed an anti-depressant. He didn't want it. No pill could fix the hole in the middle of his gut. He wanted to get past the point of mourning for what he could never have again. It hadn't happened yet.

He visited Ellen's grave every Wednesday night after he got off work, no matter the season. Amanda had activities on Wednesday night and often spent the evening with friends to allow him his night with Ellen. The rest of the week, he could pretend that life had continued, that he'd moved on as everyone encouraged. But Wednesday nights were theirs alone.

Once, he'd stopped by a bar on his way home from visiting Ellen's grave. Then having a drink after his visit became part of his routine. He'd found himself at that same bar again tonight, staring at the mug of beer in front of him. It was nearly time for him to pick up Amanda, but he was having a difficulty convincing himself to leave. He needed to straighten himself out, to work through why he couldn't stop thinking about *her*.

Sandy. He heard Althea use her name once. *Sandy*. With the full lips, the long, dark hair and the inquiring brown eyes. *Sandy*. The woman who looked at him with hesitation, but also urgency. The last time he saw her, his eyes had grazed her lips, and something foreign, but also familiar, had stirred within him. He wanted to kiss her with an intensity that shocked him. He

29

panicked. He couldn't get away fast enough. It felt like she was chasing him, breaking apart the cocoon he'd spun around his heart. He told himself he was confused and he simply needed some distance.

Then why in the hell had he bought that Santa?

He couldn't rationalize it. What was he going to do? Give it to her? What if she was involved with someone? And wasn't *he* involved with someone? He only knew that Sandy—a woman he barely knew— had made him feel alive again with a passion he thought he'd lost forever, and he had no idea what to do about it.

He couldn't return the Santa. He was afraid of seeing her, of the questions she'd have, ones for which he had no answer. The truth was he didn't want to return it. He wanted to keep it. He wanted to give it to her and see the sparkle in her eyes when she opened the box. But how could he hold onto the love for a wife he could never see again, have a girlfriend who was ready to commit to him, and still be obsessed with a stranger—a *Santa* fanatic of all things?

Man, he was losing it.

"Hey, Mac." A familiar voice mercifully broke through his loop of unanswered questions. "You okay? That beer must be warm by now."

Bill took it as a bad sign that the bartender knew his name, and, just as telling, that he knew hers. "I'm fine. Thanks. I need to get home."

He took one more sip of his nearly full beer, put some cash on the counter and stood up, venturing another glance at the woman who'd been serving him drinks every Wednesday night for more than a year.

All night long, something different about her had tickled at the back of his mind. Then it hit him. Candace had changed her hair color. She was blonde now.

Honestly, he liked her better as a redhead.

Chapter Six

Sandy

"You *sold* it?" Sandy said.

"Yes, Sandy," Althea laughed, "this is a retail store. We *sell* things."

"But I was going to *buy* it."

"In case you haven't noticed, we have a few other Santas in the store. There are plenty for you to buy." To emphasize the point, Althea placed a new recruit on the shelf, his glittery attire promising a never-ending trail of shimmery flecks across the wood floor in Sandy's house.

"But that one was unique," she argued. "There's not another one like it." Sandy scolded herself for not returning sooner. Work had been busy. She'd received another shipment of prom dresses and had been staying late at Ginger's rearranging stock for maximum exposure of the seasonal inventory. She refused to give up. She wasn't going to allow strapless special occasion dresses to stand between her and the Santa she knew was hers. "Can you see who bought it?"

"Sandy," Althea said, as if speaking to a spoiled child, which Sandy knew was appropriate, "people pass through this town on the way to somewhere else. We call them tourists. People stop here and we never see them again."

"A *tourist* bought it?" She found it offensive to think of *her* Santa with its burlap coat and leather boots in the hands of a *tourist* who likely bought it on a whim, without a thought of placement and optimal display. Sandy already had a spot on the mantel next to the surfing Santa reserved for it.

"I don't know who bought it," Althea replied, refraining from reminding her that sales to tourists kept the store open year round. "I wasn't here." She pulled another candidate from the box and freed it from the bubble wrap surrounding it.

"Can you order another one?"

Althea exhaled and set the happy fellow popping out of a chimney onto the shelf. She took the three steps to the checkout counter, placed her reading glasses on her nose and took out a binder from under the desk.

Sandy peeked through the front window at Trent. He removed his hand from the steering wheel of his Altima and made a circular movement with his index finger, urging a quick purchase. Sandy had convinced him to stop on their way to a movie—another of Sandy's attempts to add dimension to their relationship—so she could run in to pick up the prized Santa. She'd never expected it to be gone.

She smiled at Trent, and motioned for another minute.

Althea slowly turned the pages in the book, searching lists of vendors and lines of data.

While she waited, Sandy glanced at the plate of madeleines next to the coffee and hot tea Althea had available for her customers. She occupied herself by imagining them as sugar cookies shaped like bells and stars with red frosting and white sprinkles next to a container of hot chocolate. She instantly felt better.

"Sorry," Althea said. "Discontinued."

33

Sandy's blissful moment vanished.

She felt a hand on her arm, causing her to jump.

"The movie's starting soon," Trent said. "Is there a problem?"

"They *sold* it," Sandy said, her words echoing her desperation. She knew that the emotion she had attached to the object wasn't rational. She started to say they should go, but Trent had gone into problem solving mode.

"Can you order another one?" he asked Althea.

Althea pushed up her reading glasses. "Discontinued." She blinked at Trent, waiting for his next suggestion.

"Who bought it?"

Sandy expected Althea to reiterate her tourist speech. Instead, she picked up the phone. "Hey, Vicki, got a question for you."

As Althea explained the situation to her assistant, Trent drummed his fingernails on the counter. Sandy knew his habit well, but she hadn't decided if she liked it.

"You're kidding," Althea said, shaking her head and nodding at Sandy, indicating she had an answer. "Well, I never would have guessed." She hung up. "Mac bought it."

"Who's Mac?" Sandy and Trent said together.

"Oh, you've seen him, Sandy. He's always here in the snowman section. He did that great display last year at his house on the west side of town. I don't remember him ever buying a Santa before."

The room suddenly became very small. Sandy flushed at the realization that the other object of her affection had purchased *her* Santa.

"There you go, Sandy," Trent said. "*Mac* bought it. If you're that attached to the Santa, maybe you can ask him about it the next time you see him." He was still solving the problem.

Sandy's face flamed. "It's okay. I'm not that attached. We can go." Even as she said the words, she knew she wasn't telling the truth. She was attached, and she wasn't talking about a small statue with a burlap coat and leather boots. "We can go."

Trent extended his long arm to pluck an ornament from one of the display trees. "Do you like this one?" He held a blown glass ornament with a painting of the smiling Santa.

"It's pretty." And it was. She had several like it at home.

Trent pulled out his wallet and handed Althea a twenty. She could almost hear him say, "Mission accomplished," as if any Santa would do.

Sandy appreciated the effort, but not all Santas were the same, and there was a man out there somewhere named Mac who knew the difference.

Chapter Seven

Bill

Bill took a moment to observe Amanda before going in for their nightly check-in. She lay across her bed, her eyes focused on the pages of her geometry book. Next to her was a plate of half-eaten lasagna. She had put on a little weight, adding an inch or two as he had. Bill couldn't blame it all on Gwen's cooking and her desire to nurture them. Amanda had inherited his body type, more on the sturdy side rather than less slender the way Ellen had been. It was one thing for a thirty-seven-year-old man to have less than the perfect physique, but it had to be difficult for a teenager. He didn't know how to talk to her about it, so he encouraged her love of sports, bought her whole-grain snack bars and took her out for fruit smoothies. Tonight, she'd pulled her blondish-brown hair into a ponytail, allowing him the illusion that she was still a little girl. She was growing up too fast.

She looked up. "Hey, Dad. You okay?"

He cleared his thoughts. "Sure, honey. Just wondering how my best girl is doing in geometry."

"If your *best girl* is Trisha Martin," she joked, "she's doing great."

Bill laughed as he lowered himself into Amanda's beanbag chair. He had argued for a nice big easy chair, one where he could plant himself and stay for hours in the shelter of her room.

The clever teenager had made his visiting spot as uncomfortable as possible without placing tacks in the seat. She needed her space. Bill knew it, but he wasn't willing to give up their chats, not without a fight.

Amanda closed her book, seemingly resigning herself to her father's presence. "So how's it going with you, Dad?" She took another bite of the leftover lasagna that Gwen had made the night before. If Gwen's nurturing continued, they'd all be as round as his snow families.

"I've been working on the mischievous snowman, or should I say, the snowman acting in self-defense. I mean the kid did steal his nose. I want him to be the feature in this year's display, but he may not be up for the limelight. The rate it's going, he might be stuffed in the side yard with the reindeer."

She chewed on the side of her lip. "You *do* know this is March, right?"

"Yes, I know." If he didn't know, he'd have Gwen—and now Amanda—to remind him.

"Dad," she said in her "we're both adults" voice, "we don't have to do the big Christmas display this year."

Bill nodded slowly, indicating he was listening, a technique he'd learned in a counseling session.

"I was thinking," she continued, "we could just put up a tree instead, or maybe we can go skiing."

"We can go skiing, if you'd like. I might have to make a few trips to the gym before then." He laughed, trying to lighten her mood. "But where's all this coming from?"

"Mom. . ." Her voice caught. "Mom wouldn't mind if we didn't do the display."

He took in the earnest face of his daughter. She had his hazel eyes, but the cute, upturned nose was all Ellen. He could almost see Ellen standing there with her hands on her hips. "Mac," she would say when she snuck a lighted reindeer into his village, "I'm only adding a little color to our snowdrifts." Bill had always preferred the relaxed nature of snowmen that existed at the whim of the elements and could never take themselves too seriously. He had come to envy their contented state of being. "The display was always more my thing than hers."

"You had fun together. I remember." Amanda sat up and shifted to the edge of her bed, emphasizing the importance of her words. "You know I like helping with the snow village, but Gwen doesn't get it. Maybe it would be better if we did something different this year."

He hated that Amanda could feel the tension between him and Gwen. Lately, his emotions had been closer to the surface, and he was finding it more difficult to maintain an outwardly even temperament. "Sure. We can talk about it later. We have plenty of time. You *do* know this is March, right?"

He had hoped for a laugh, but Amanda tucked in her lower lip, a sign she was weighing her words carefully.

"Go ahead," he said. "You can talk to me." Encouraging dialogue was another technique he'd learned in counseling.

"So I was in your room, borrowing socks—thanks for those, by the way—and I decided I'd hang up some of the shirts on your bed. You know if you hang them up right after you take them out of the dryer, they won't get so wrinkled."

He held back a smile. "I appreciate the advice."

"Anyway, I noticed the Althea's bag in the closet. I'm sorry I snooped, but I wanted to see the new snowman we'd be adding to our collection. But, Dad, it's a *Santa*! You never buy Santas. Is it a present for Gwen?"

"For Gwen?" Bill stammered. "No. It's for . . ." He shook his head, completely baffled by his own actions. "I don't know. It's just something I bought."

"You're not losing it or anything, are you?"

She had echoed his thoughts. He might be losing it, just not how Amanda imagined. "I think I'll be able to hold it together a while longer."

She let out a sigh, which he assumed was relief. "I've been thinking about the Santa. The boots are real leather and the jacket has wool trim. Mom would have liked it. Is that why you bought it?"

Bill hadn't thought about his desire to buy the Santa in terms of Ellen, but he could see it now. He imagined her placing it on the mantel and stepping back to observe it. "Oh, Mac," he could almost hear in her sweet voice, "he's just what the family needs."

"Yes," he agreed. "Your mom would have liked it." He only wished he'd been thinking of Ellen when he bought it.

He needed a distraction. "Hey, how about this? Just you and me. We take a little trip this weekend. We can head into Lafayette, go to your favorite restaurant, see your grandma and grandpa if you'd like, and I'll even make the supreme sacrifice and take you to the mall."

Her eyes narrowed. "You want to see Grandma and Grandpa and take me to the mall? You sure you're not losing it?"

"I'm sure that I'd like to spend time with you."

"Okay, Dad, but I'm picking the music for the ride."

He groaned, just to make a show of it. He did want more time with Amanda, but he also hoped that time away from St. Clair might help him break the spell of a brown-eyed beauty that threatened to invade his heart.

Chapter Eight

❄ ❄ ❄

Sandy

Sandy cut a red and white striped Grand Perfection tulip from the garden bed in front of her porch, grateful she'd purchased her house in time to plant bulbs last fall. During recent weeks, she'd marveled at the stems peeking through, then the buds, and finally this vibrant display of multi-colors dancing in the breeze. The hours she'd spent on her knees with a trowel in hand last fall had been worth it to make the festival of spring happen.

"Oh yes," she said to a clump of daffodils, "I haven't forgotten you." She clipped several of the yellow beauties and added them to her bouquet, thinking how much her grandfather, Art Morgan, would have loved her blooming garden. Spring—April in particular—had been his favorite time of year. He had organized the St. Clair Annual Garden Tour and personally greeted the visitors before they meandered through the curved paths of their backyard bursting with lilacs, sweet peas, azaleas, tulips, and daffodils. Her grandmother, Virgie,—whom she had called by her first name since she was a child, copying how Candace had addressed her—had continued the tradition of opening the garden to a parade of delighted spring enthusiasts.

Both she and Virgie could look forward to the garden tour once they made it through today.

A familiar horn sounded. Virgie pulled up to the curb in her grandfather's beloved car. Sandy thought he had purchased the British antique simply so he could have a sign in his garage that read, "Art's Morgan." The sign was still there and the luxury car remained in its bay except for those special occasions when it made a public appearance. Today was one of those days—the first anniversary of Art's death—and they were going to visit him at his grave near the stone angel in the center of St. Clair Memorial Cemetery. When he had purchased the cemetery plots years ago, he'd told Virgie, "If I leave this world before you, I won't have your pretty face to see every day. That angel will keep me company."

"So there'll be *another woman*," Virgie had joked. "I'll have to keep an eye on you." After forty years of marriage, keeping an eye on him was a habit she wasn't ready to break.

Sandy slid into the soft camel-colored leather seats of the burgundy-colored Morgan, placing her hand on the wooden dashboard, cradling the bouquet on her lap. She leaned over and planted a kiss on Virgie's wrinkled cheek.

Virgie was wearing Art's favorite colors in the form of a floral scarf and burgundy cashmere sweater—to match the Morgan, of course—and a rosy lipstick.

"I see the convertible has been converted," Sandy said. Art only drove his prize on days when he could ride with the top down. Virgie preferred a less breezy excursion with the top in place, but this was Art's day, and somehow he had arranged for sunshine and warmer temperatures to encourage their open-air trek.

"Occasionally," Virgie said, "I have to let the old fool have his way. Will your mother be joining us?" She flipped her scarf from one side to the other, going for nonchalant, as if she were indifferent to her only daughter's absence.

"She said she'd bring by some flowers later," Sandy offered. Candace wasn't much for ceremony, particularly ones that might involve emotion. She'd barely made it through Art's funeral before finding a reason to escape.

"I hope it isn't lilies, Virgie said. "Art hated lilies."

Sandy considered correcting her grandmother. Art didn't *hate* any flower. Lilies just hadn't made it on to his list of favorites. Sandy doubted Candace had taken note of Art's favorites since she thought he had designed the backyard to be her personal tanning bed. Sandy made a mental note to call Candace to head off the appearance of any unsightly lilies.

"I think she's bringing roses."

"Roses." Virgie narrowed her blue eyes, likely looking for some fault with roses. Finding none, she smiled at Sandy's bouquet. "Art will be pleased that you brought flowers from your garden. Your house looks pretty with all the tulips and daffodils blooming."

Sandy also took in the view of her small, brick home. "It does, doesn't it?"

She loved her house, which had nestled itself in among similar post-war models, heavy on charm, light on space. The location near downtown and her job had been a selling point. Its inconveniences—a one-car garage, only one full bathroom located upstairs and a pantry the size of a shoebox—could not detract from the tug of living in an older home, one with the history and character that newer homes could never achieve.

She focused on the two glazed pots that flanked her staircase. They were bright and cheerful, brimming with the purple cyclamen and alyssum she had purchased from the nursery. "Trent helped me with the planters," she said, recalling the day last fall when Trent had driven her to Lafayette to choose them. He was patient with her extended shopping process and made jokes about the weight of the pots sending him to the hospital. They were happy then. Maybe they could be happy again. "He's very helpful," Sandy added, more to herself than to Virgie.

Virgie patted Sandy's leg, as if she knew Trent might need a vote in his favor. She waited another minute and then hit the gas pedal. The Morgan lurched forward, quickly picking up speed. Virgie and Candace were different in many ways—Virgie, proper and reserved, Candace, carefree and easy—but when it came to driving, they had taken lessons at the same racetrack. Sandy gathered her hair at the base of her neck and held on.

They turned onto Main Street, greeted by the honks and waves that always accompanied the Morgan's outings. They passed Althea's, and Sandy couldn't stop herself from wishing she might catch a glimpse of her favorite customer. She assumed he wouldn't be there since it was the middle of the day and he likely worked—somewhere—but the thought of him laughing at a dancing snowman brought a smile. Of course, the snowman in her mind was in *her* home and the one laughing at him was sitting beside her on her couch in front of a fire.

Sandy caught herself. That fantasy was not going to help find her way back to a happy place with Trent. She needed to think of a future with the man currently in her life. She had purchased her house with the thought of a family and everything they could share in their home. She was already planning future holidays. Thanksgiving dinners and a New Year's Eve toast. On Christmas mornings, they'd unwrap presents followed by a breakfast of pancakes and sausages. In the evening, friends and family would gather there for dinner with a tour of holiday lights with wine and hot toddies after. When she bought her house, she believed it was all possible.

"I love my house, Virgie. You'll never know how grateful I am to you and Art for helping me."

"Helping you what?" Without lifting her foot form gas pedal, Virgie took the curve around the City Park to the road that lead to the cemetery. Sandy imagined her popping wheelies when she was young.

Sandy dug her fingers deeper into the leather armrest. "Purchase my house. You knew I used money from my trust fund for the down payment."

"Yes, I knew, but..." She braked for a four-way stop. With no other cars at the intersection, Sandy expected a heavy foot on the gas pedal for the takeoff but Virgie hesitated, drumming her fingers on the steering wheel. "Is that what Candace told you? That Art and I helped with your trust fund?"

"Candace didn't mention you specifically. Her name was the only one listed as Trustee, but the amount was substantial enough, I assumed you and Art had contributed."

Virgie tightened her lips, the way she did when she was measuring her words. "Of course, you'll have your inheritance, but you don't need to thank Art or me for your fund. You need to thank your father."

"My father?"

Virgie opened her mouth and closed it as quickly.

"But he was a surfer," Sandy said. "Do surfers have money?"

Virgie glared at her rearview mirror and then sped away.

Sandy pressed on. "Candace told me about the fund when I was twenty-one. She said she would have told me earlier, but I

44

didn't need it for college since Art had paid for my course in fashion merchandising. I knew it was too much money for my mother to save by herself. I always thought you and Art were involved."

Virgie made an effort to keep her eyes focused on some distant point.

If Sandy had been driving, she would have pulled to the side of the road and held Virgie hostage until she had answers. As it was, Virgie had full control of the car…and the information.

Sandy sighed with frustration. As she had for most of her life, her family had left her to draw her own conclusions. As far as she knew, Sander Jones, award winning California surfer, had given her his name and nothing else. He existed as some photos and newspaper clippings. Candace said he couldn't be part of their lives, so Sandy never expected anything from him. She'd always believed the reason he couldn't be with them was never about her or Candace, but some unnamed force that kept them apart. Now there was money between them. He may have given it out of guilt, or love, or because the court ordered it, but it was there now, in the form of brick, leaded-glass windows, oak floors and a mortgage she could afford.

Everything Sandy thought she knew about her father was now in jeopardy. She had come to terms with never knowing him, but maybe she'd given up too easily.

"Is Candace still in touch with him? She told me she didn't know where he lived."

Virgie offered a sympathetic glance. "I'm sorry, but you'll need to discuss it with your mother."

"A discussion would imply that two people are opening their mouths." Sandy could feel an old anger bubbling to the surface. "When it comes to the topic of my father, Candace's lips are superglued."

"Then unglue them. It's time, Sandy." The tone of her voice said she'd given all the clues she was willing to give. She'd opened the door. Sandy would now need to walk through it on her own.

For the rest of the silent ride, Sandy was lost in a jumble of her own thoughts. Virgie seemed equally unsettled.

They drove through the arch that marked the cemetery's entrance and passed a section reserved for infants and children. At the sight of the tiny graves decorated with teddy bears and balloons, Sandy closed her eyes and wished peace for the parents who would never see their little ones dance and play. Such a stark loss made a distant father seem insignificant.

Virgie pulled into the designated parking area and allowed the Morgan to idle. They both took a moment to adjust to the setting. Sandy assumed Virgie's thoughts mirrored her own. Art should be at home, sitting in his big leather chair in his office, wearing his favorite slippers and reading the latest spy novel. But he was here, in a place far away, when he'd always been so close.

Virgie turned off the engine and it sputtered in protest. They opened their car doors. Sandy gently shut hers, while Virgie allowed hers to close with a thud. They both stepped onto the gravel path lined with boxwoods trimmed to a uniform size. Art would have given the gardener a pat on the back. The noise under their feet seemed too loud, an intrusion on the quiet solitude. Sandy moved to the grass while Virgie crunched on.

At Art's grave, Sandy laid her bouquet on the ground. A few petals from the tulips broke free and the breeze carried them to the next grave. Virgie knelt and rearranged some lilacs already in the vase on his headstone, adding cherry blossoms she'd cut from a tree in her backyard.

The cherry tree was another sign of spring, one that Art cherished. She missed him. When he was alive, Sandy didn't have an overwhelming need to connect with her father. Recently, though, Sander Jones had been occupying her thoughts, with unanswered questions seeking answers. She could now see that the surfing Santa on her mantel had been a beginning. Without realizing it, she had already been reaching toward her father.

She heard a flutter in the breeze. She followed the whir to a red and yellow plastic pinwheel. Someone had inserted the toy into a bouquet of daisies set on a grave across from the stone angel. The wheel spun again in the breeze, reminding her of the pinwheel ornaments that she and Art had made when she was a child. He had patiently watched as Sandy cut the fabric into triangles and then helped her glue on the buttons that held them together. If he could send her a message, one that said he agreed with Virgie that it was time, that spinning wheel would be the way.

Candace might not be ready to tell her story, but Sandy needed to know the truth. She knew what she had to do.

Chapter Nine

Candace
Thirty-one plus years ago

Nineteen-year-old Candace Silva stretched her arms and legs and yawned. She felt as content as a cat sitting in the sun, which made it difficult to convince herself it was time to leave. She might have had more success if she knew where she wanted to go. She'd been in Los Angeles for twenty-four hours and had only managed a walk on the beach and a stroll through the Huntington Beach Surfing Museum. Then she'd landed on the patio of a restaurant simply called "The Cantina," and had stayed for two hours, feasting on the best Mexican food she'd ever tasted. She'd finished two bowls of chips and salsa with a side of guacamole, devoured a chicken taco, and inhaled a side of rice and beans. Add in the sunshine and the salty mist, she could see herself staying in that spot forever.

A month earlier, a classmate had returned from spring break with stories of warm sand under her feet, sunsets over the ocean, and waking to the sound of the surf outside her hotel window. She'd also gushed over the hard-bodied surfers that seemingly hung out in every local restaurant, shop, and street corner. After Candace had decided time away was what she needed, Los Angeles, specifically Huntington Beach, had become her destination. She was calling it a vacation, but the fact that she had dropped all of her classes at Lafayette Community College before she left opened the door for something more.

College had never suited her. She hated the structure and had no idea where a degree might take her. Sitting in classes had felt like high school all over again but lacked the fun of cheerleading, dances, and finding new ways of getting into trouble. Now she was free to plan her life, if she could only get out of her chair.

She wrinkled her nose as she examined the "to do" list she'd jotted down a paper napkin. She still needed to call Art and Virgie and let them know she was in LA. Candace had decided she'd break them into her news slowly. None of what she had to say to them would put her on the Nice List for Christmas. She'd spent most of the last few years on the other List anyway. Too many nights of sneaking out and coming home late had put her on semi-permanent lockdown.

Their relationship had improved when she'd gone away to college, about the same time she had also begun addressing her mother by her first name. Candace had said it once when she didn't want her roommate to know her mother had called *again*. It felt right, so she'd continued. Virgie accepted the change in title, almost as if it had lifted some of the burden of playing the mother role. They seemed to make better friends than they did mother and daughter. One phone call and the "friendship" she'd established with her mother and stepfather could take a serious hit.

She folded the napkin, giving it a sharp crease across the middle. She'd make that call tomorrow. This afternoon, she needed to concentrate on tracking down a local hotel. She'd booked one more night in the motel by the airport, but being in a flight path next to a highway wasn't her idea of a restful night's sleep.

Candace took one last drink through her straw, making a slurping sound, drawing the attention of one of the guys sitting at the bar. Actually, she'd had his attention for the past hour. He exuded a beach vibe, with flip-flops, battered cargo shorts, a t-shirt that hung on him, rumpled blond hair and an even tan. He also had a contagious laugh that he shared with his friends and an easy pace that she noticed when he walked in. He was attractive, she supposed, if she cared about attractive right now.

The waitress delivered her check. Candace picked it up and reached for her purse. A hand plucked the check from her. She looked up into blue eyes and a welcoming smile.

"Why don't you let me take care of this?" Mr. Beach Vibe asked in a tone slow enough to win a label of "drawl."

"Why would you do that?"

"Because having you here has made my afternoon, and I'd really like to pay for that taco."

"Only the taco?" She should have protested, but he seemed friendly enough.

"I'll also cover half the beans, a third of the rice, and several scoops of the guacamole. You're on your own for the chips."

"The chips are free."

"Guess it's your lucky day." He pulled out a chair, swung it around and sat down.

"Well, just make yourself at home," she joked.

"Why thank you." He held the check in the air. The waitress grabbed it as she was passing by. He grinned. "I have a tab."

Candace liked the creases at the corners of his eyes and his confidence. "Thanks."

He folded his arms over the back of the chair. "He didn't show up?"

"Who?"

"The one you've been waiting for."

A flush rose to her face. "A girl can't eat a taco by herself?"

"A girl can, but it seems like a waste of a good chair." He stared at her, the grin never leaving his face, as if she would tell her life story to a stranger who had invited himself into her space.

"I'm not waiting for anyone," she said, after his stare became uncomfortable.

"Good. Later tonight, if you're hungry again, maybe I could take you out for something more interesting than a taco and we could try out a couple of new chairs. There's a restaurant in Laguna Beach that sits on the cliff above the beach with a nice view. It's called 'The Breeze.' Do you know it?"

She didn't want to tell him that she'd only arrived yesterday and her LA restaurant experience was limited to fast food and this place. "Can't say that I do."

"It's pretty there. Since you're a fan of patios, you'll like it. I spend a lot of time in the ocean. It's good to get a view from above. Gives you a different perspective."

Candace couldn't argue with a different perspective. She'd flown across the country to get a different perspective, but she'd planned on doing it alone. "You're asking me out? You don't know anything about me."

"I know you're from Indiana, or at least you're a fan." He motioned to her shirt.

She glanced down at the black and gold letters that read *Purdue*. She'd never been a fan, but the t-shirt had found its way into her suitcase and onto her body this morning, reminding her that even two thousand miles couldn't separate her from her life.

"Did you go to school there?" he asked.

She shook her head. "The shirt was a gift." She decided to put it back in her suitcase and keep it there. She couldn't leave everything behind, but she didn't have to wear around a reminder.

His grin faded slightly. "A gift." He blinked several times with eyelashes that demanded attention and appeared to consider her further. "I'd still take you for a Midwest girl. So, what do you say? Will you have dinner with me tonight?"

She placed her elbows on the table. "I'll think about it if you tell me about Eddie."

He lightly touched his worn black t-shirt with the words, "What would Eddie do?" written in white letters. "You must be new in town. Eddie Aikua is famous in this crowd." He pushed the blonde curls away from his forehead, which only added to his appeal. "Eddie was a champion surfer and lifeguard at Waimea Bay on Oahu. He made rescues in impossible situations, and he tackled the big waves no one else would. When you can't decide whether you want to go for it or take the easy way out, you can ask yourself—"

"What would Eddie do?" Candace finished. She didn't see an easy way out, and "going for it" in either direction would likely create a new set of problems. Maybe she'd move into this little space on the patio and live here forever. "So, what happened to brave Eddie?"

He laughed and the crinkles next to his eyes deepened. "Died on a rescue mission. Rescuing people is risky business." He raised his eyebrows, surveying her carefully.

She crossed her arms over her chest. "I don't need rescuing, if that's what you're thinking."

"Maybe I'm the one who needs to be rescued."

She doubted it, but she liked him for saying it. "So you surf."

"I do. I surf competitively. I have a sponsor, so practice is my middle name. I need to get in another run this evening."

Candace couldn't imagine surfing being an actual job, but she *was* new in town.

He laughed again. "I can see you're not impressed. I also have an accounting business on the side. Seems I'm good with numbers. The Cantina here is one of my clients."

"Do they pay you in beer and nachos?"

"No way," the waitress interrupted on her way past their table. "We'd be bankrupt within a week,"

He waved her away. "I do enjoy an occasional beer, but I never drink before I surf. You have to respect the water. I have been known to nacho, however." He smiled. "Why don't you come with me? I can set you up on the beach with a new chair and you can take in the sunset. It's the best part of the day."

She drew back. "I really hadn't planned on socializing tonight."

His smile dropped like a sad puppy dog. "I guess we could make it another time. May I call you tomorrow?"

"That might be difficult since my phone is in Indiana."

"I knew a Midwest girl when I saw one." He reached in his pocket, pulled out his wallet, and placed his card on the table. "While you're here, consider me at your service. I offer restaurant critiques, taxi service, and surf lessons; plus, I can do your taxes."

She picked up the card and read it. *Sander Jones. Certified Public Accountant.* "A CPA. Impressive. Did your mother name you Sander?"

"Nope. My first surf-instructor, Big Dog Jenkins, gave everyone a nickname. I just happened to like his name better than the one my mother gave me. And what does your mother call you?"

She had to give him points. He'd found a clever way to get her name. "She calls me Candace." She smiled. "Among other things."

"All right, Candace from Indiana, I won't make you socialize if that's not what you want, but keep my card and call me if you need anything. I might be a good man to know." He stood up and flipped his chair around. In a minute, he would be out the door on the way to his next surfing run.

"I could use a recommendation for a hotel," she said quickly. "Some place quiet and inexpensive and not too far from the ocean. Is that possible?"

He grinned again. "I know just the spot. Tell you what. Come with me to the beach and watch the sunset and I'll find you a good place to settle while you're here."

He was asking her to trust him. Despite wanting to remain distant, he was drawing her in. "I suppose I could try out a new chair."

She picked up the napkin with her "to do" list. Before dropping it into her purse, she unfolded it, grabbed her pen and wrote, "Watch the sunset." Tomorrow would be soon enough to figure out the rest of her life.

Summer

Chapter Ten

Sandy

Sandy added a new stars and stripes bulb to her ornament tree already sporting glass versions of Uncle Sam and Betsy Ross. She repositioned a little wooden flag and stepped back to enjoy her patriotic display, stopping short of saluting. She might have done it as a joke, if Trent had been in a joking mood. He'd tuned his Pandora to smooth jazz and proceeded to chop the vegetables in silence, his concentration complete. In spite of her efforts to shake up their routine, their Tuesday night stay-at-home dinners had continued as if they had a life of their own. She placed a red, white, and blue star on top of the tree and returned to the kitchen.

She began tearing the romaine for the salad, shooting Trent a sideways glance. Since he'd arrived, he'd been preoccupied. Given his mood, Sandy considered not sharing her news, but she wanted to tell *someone*, and it was too soon to discuss with Virgie. Candace was definitely out.

"I hired a private investigator to find my father."

"Your father?" The rhythm of Trent's chop continued uninterrupted. "The guy who abandoned you?"

"Maybe he didn't abandon me. You know Candace. It's possible that while she was tossing suitcases into her Mazda RX7, he was paddling out to the waves and didn't have a clue."

"And what if he was? Do you even know if he's still alive?"

"I don't know, but he would only be in his fifties so I have to assume he's still with us. And if he is, I'd like to talk to him. He put money into an account for me and I want to thank him."

"Fathers are *supposed* to give money to their kids. They have laws about these things. Why do you need to find him now? You've made it thirty years without knowing him." He pushed the chopped cucumber, red onion, and peppers to the side of the cutting board and started on the carrots.

Sandy wished she had an answer that would satisfy Trent. She didn't feel lost without her father. She simply wanted to *know* him, to find out if they shared common interests. She wanted to find out what he liked for breakfast and how he took his coffee, if he even drank coffee. Maybe he had other children. *Her brothers and sisters.* She wanted to meet them. She'd love to have siblings. Since both she and Candace were only children, their family tree was barely a bush. She also wanted to locate her father for Candace. Sandy wasn't foolish enough to believe they'd fall into each others' arms or they would all suddenly become a real family, but she believed Candace *needed* to reconnect with Sander Jones, if only to let him go for good. As Virgie had said, now was the time.

She exhaled, building renewed conviction. "The point is he has a story, one I'd like to hear, not Candace's edited version. Virgie and Art were never any help. Whenever I asked them about Sander, all they would say was that the timing wasn't right for them, but that he'd been a good person who loved me. You have both of your parents, Trent. You don't know how it feels to know there's someone out there, someone important, whom you've never met."

"I have tons of cousins I've never met and I don't care."

"Cousins are different than a father."

He shrugged and kept chopping. "A stranger is a stranger."

She wanted to argue, but their arguments were more like intellectual discussions that left her exhausted. "Is that a new shirt?" she asked instead, studying the button-up cotton shirt with a blue and gold abstract print. "I like it, but it's a little out of character for you." Trent tended to stick with grays and browns, and, in the winter, his argyle sweater for variety. Now was the season for his collection of T-shirts with computer code that she assumed had some sort of joke imbedded in them. This shirt was definitely not Trent, or at least not the Trent she knew.

"Maybe my character is changing."

Something was changing, but she doubted it was Trent's character. He'd cut his mop of hair, which could mean a job interview. He hadn't mentioned a promotion, but during recent weeks, he'd gone silent on his usual grumble about the office and his co-workers. "How are things at work?"

"Good," he said noncommittally.

"Anything happening?"

"Like what?" He chopped the last of the carrots and scanned for more. They already had enough to feed a small family of rabbits.

She assumed no promotion, but there was something. "Didn't you get a new team member?"

Sandy had never seen Trent blush, but his cheeks appeared to be taking on some new color. "Frankie came on board a few weeks ago. Losing Reynaldo set the project timeline back, but Frankie's a quick study and we're almost on track."

"Frankie? As in Frank or Francesca?"

"We all call her Frankie," he replied defensively.

"Does *Frankie* like your new shirt?" Sandy was teasing, but Trent kept his eyes on the chopping board. She would have continued with her questions, but she didn't like the direction the conversation had taken. She was feeling off-balance, and Trent seemed equally anxious. It would have been the perfect time for them to have a conversation about their relationship. Instead, Sandy took the opportunity to interject her plan. "Since we're changing character here," she said, "I thought we might do something different for Fourth of July this year."

"The Fourth?" Color rose again in his cheeks. "Yes, I was going to talk to you about it."

"You were?" She doubted their ideas on the "something different" were the same. Since they'd been together, they had celebrated the Fourth in the courtyard of Trent's apartment building where they would drink wine with his neighbors while they caught a glimpse of the city fireworks display in the distance. This year, she wanted to be closer to the action.

"I think it would be fun to go to the city picnic," she said. "We can go early and get a good spot on the lawn. We'll be close to the fireworks and we'll be able to hear the music."

It had been years since she'd attended the Fourth of July celebration. Virgie had taken her as a child, and she'd gone with friends as a teenager. Nostalgia may have been the motivation she'd share with Trent, but her real motivation wasn't nearly as innocent.

She hoped to see *him*. Pathetic, she knew, but their last meeting felt unfinished. Since then, he'd disappeared—with *her* Santa. Now he had a name—*Mac*—although he didn't seem like a Mac. But he had a name, and she knew it. She thought she upped her chances of seeing him by attending an event for the entire town. She almost hoped she saw him with his wife so she could move on. Maybe she could even wrestle her favorite Santa away from him before saying her final goodbye.

"It's a family event, Sandy. There'll be kids everywhere." Trent only liked kids in small quantities, mainly his niece and nephew who had reached the age where reasoning was possible. "Jason's having a barbecue. I thought I might go."

"Jason? The guy from the QA department? I thought he made you crazy. And since when do you socialize with people from work?" Even as she asked the question, she was forming an answer.

I thought I might go. He'd never intended to invite her. For a reason that was becoming obvious, he wanted to make his appearance as an unattached man. A seed of panic took root. She'd been fantasizing about a married man under the safety net of her relationship with Trent. Did he suspect, or was this distraction his own? She could pull him back, invite herself to the barbecue, let go of the man she only knew as Mac. She needed to stop obsessing, to get her life back before it was too late. "Trent, I . . ." The buzzer went off on the oven. Whatever words she might have said were lost in the sound.

He held out his hand for Sandy's bowl of lettuce. She slid it toward him and he dumped his vegetable garden on top. She'd be eating salad for a week.

Sandy opened the oven door, pulled out the baked salmon and silently dished it onto their plates. She added a side of rice and a serving of salad.

Trent opened the bottle of *fumé blanc*, the same variety of wine they drank whenever they had salmon, a regular on their Tuesday night menu. He poured the wine, sliced a lemon and squirted it onto the fish, finishing with a twist of pepper, repeating the same sequence of actions she had seen for the last two years. She wondered how many more years they would follow the same pattern and if the sameness would continue to wear on her. She sometimes had difficulty remembering the early days when it all seemed simple. They'd started dating and continued, not as much because they were passionate about their future together, but because nothing had interrupted them. Now interruptions seemed impossible to ignore. She simultaneously welcomed them and feared them. But they were here, and both she and Trent had to find out where they would lead.

"I think the barbecue sounds like a good idea," she said. "I hope you don't mind if I attend the picnic. Virgie might like to go."

He looked up. The anxiety had disappeared. "I don't mind." He set their plates on a tray and carried them to the dining room.

Sandy picked up their wine glasses and followed him so they could complete their Tuesday routine.

Chapter Eleven

Amanda

Amanda was a good sport. Her dad always said so. Sometimes being a good sport meant she did what adults wanted her to do. Today was one of those days.

Her dad had made his plea last week.

"Gwen wants to take you out for your birthday," he'd said. "I was hoping you'd let your old man off the hook by picking out your own presents." He'd already paid for volleyball camp, and had a party planned with her friends, which was great, but she thought he was doing too much. Now she had a whole afternoon with Gwen. She was nice, but Amanda thought she was mainly being nice because she wanted her dad to like her. He did like her, but he didn't love her. Amanda could tell.

For lunch, they'd gone to The Bistro, Gwen's choice. They'd eaten soup and salad with iced tea to drink. As Amanda finished her salad and tea, wishing she had a burger and a coke, Gwen informed her they'd be going to a local women's clothing store to shop for her birthday presents.

"I like H&M," Amanda said, "and Forever 21. Maybe we can drive into Lafayette and go to the mall."

Gwen made a pretense of considering the option before continuing to sell her idea. "Ginger's has a nice selection of junior clothing. And it's *quality* clothing. It's your birthday. You should have something special."

"But isn't it expensive?"

"Mac said you wouldn't want to spend the money. I've never known such a practical teenager. My nieces would have already spent it and come back for more. Practical is good, but you can splurge a little."

"I'm saving for college."

"He said you didn't have to worry about college, and he wants you to have something now."

Since her mother's death, her dad had become more "live for the moment" with less focus on the future. *Enjoy life today* had become his favorite saying, which was funny since he didn't seem to be enjoying much of today at all. But if spending his money on over-priced clothes would make him happy, she'd play along.

They walked into the store and a sales clerk with pink streaked hair immediately offered them a high-pitched, "Welcome to Ginger's." Amanda recognized her as a graduate from her high school, probably making some money before she went away to college. Amanda planned to go away to college, but her dad would want her to come home for the summers. She might be able to get a job at a place like Ginger's. Maybe Gwen had been right to choose this place. She did feel more adult here. After all, she was turning fifteen.

The girl continued to sort clothes, and Amanda thought she could use some work on her customer service skills. Another greeting followed, this time from a woman with long, dark hair with a nametag that read, "Sandy," and identified her as the manager. She wore an ivory colored suit with a flared jacket and straight skirt that reminded Amanda of something her grandmother would wear, only because it looked expensive. Her grandmother liked expensive.

"Nice to see you again," Sandy, the Manager, said to Gwen. "You came in a few months ago. How did the coat work out?"

Gwen looked more suspicious than impressed. "You remember me and the coat I bought?"

Amanda *was* impressed. She couldn't imagine a salesperson at Forever 21 remembering any customer, and definitely not a purchase.

"It was a lovely herringbone and one of my favorite pieces of that collection," Sandy said.

"Oh, well, thank you. It worked out. That's why I've brought Amanda in today. It's her birthday."

Amanda cringed. Gwen seemed to want to tell the world it was her birthday, as if they would both receive extra points. She waited for Sandy to say *Happy Birthday!* That's what everyone said when Gwen told them.

Sandy tilted her head slightly. "Sixteen?"

"Fifteen."

"Fifteen." Sandy's brown eyes actually seem to sparkle. Amanda had heard about eyes "sparkling" before, but she'd never seen it. "Aw, it's your Quinceañera."

"I guess it is. What's my Quinceañera?"

"It's your fifteenth birthday celebration. According to Latin American tradition, a girl's fifteen birthday is her coming-of-age and they celebrate with a huge party. When I was a high school, I had friend whose family was from Mexico and they threw a party for her. She wore a strapless, beaded ballgown. It was so beautiful. I wanted one of my own." She laughed. "I still do. And it's not only the dress. The girl gives a candle to each of the fifteen people she considers the most important in her life. It's tradition."

"I don't know if I could think of fifteen people," Amanda said.

"Oh, you could," Sandy said. "Your parents, your grandparents, teachers, friends. Once you start thinking, you'll want more than fifteen candles."

Amanda turned to Gwen. "Can we get some candles?"

"We could, but you're not from Mexico, and your party's at Pizza Haven, so I can't see giving out candles."

Amanda still wanted candles. She wondered if she'd use one of her candles for Gwen, and instantly felt guilty for the thought. She probably needed a candle. Maybe two.

Sandy smiled at Gwen, but Amanda bet she was forcing it. "I know you're here for Amanda," Sandy said, "but I think I have the perfect blouse for you." She stepped to a rack and pulled out an electric blue satin blouse. She held it up for Gwen. "It's very flattering."

Gwen touched the sleeve.

"It's pretty," Amanda said. "Try it on. I need to look around anyway."

Gwen made a show of reluctance, but took the blouse anyway and disappeared into the dressing room.

Sandy moved closer to Amanda and whispered. "It's nice you're spending time you're your mom on your birthday. I'm sure she appreciates it."

"She's not my mom," Amanda said abruptly. "She's my dad's girlfriend."

Sandy nodded. She probably thought her parents were divorced, like Lacey's, but Amanda's dad would never have divorced her mom. Her parents would have been married forever.

"My mom died in a car accident," Amanda said before she realized the words were out.

Sandy's mouth form for silent *oh*. Amanda waited for her to say, "I'm sorry," because that's what everyone always said to make her feel better, or maybe because they didn't know what else to say.

"I'm sure your mother would have liked to have been here for your birthday. I bet she'd want you to have a wonderful present. Let's find something good."

She began pulling clothes from the racks, holding shirts in front of Amanda, finding some acceptable while rejecting others. She pulled an empty rack from the side and began filling it. Gwen came out of the dressing room wearing the blue blouse, tugging at it.

"You don't love it," Sandy said. She pinched the sides of the blouse at the waist. "You might need a smaller size."

The idea of a smaller size seemed to have Gwen reconsidering the blouse.

"Perhaps you'd prefer a different color. An emerald green would accent your eyes. If Amanda would like to choose a few more things, you can try on everything together."

Amanda took the prompt and grabbed some jeans.

Sandy pulled the green blouse, added a floral skirt, and handed them to Gwen before she had a chance to reject them. "Do you like dresses?" she asked Amanda.

"She never wears dresses," Gwen answered over her shoulder as she headed back to the dressing room. Amanda wanted to say it wasn't true. She used to wear dresses; she just hadn't worn any lately. She wished Gwen would stop speaking for her.

"Why don't you try a few sundresses?" Sandy said. "It's always good to have at least one in your closet." She went to a circular rack and pulled two dresses to add to Amanda's selections. "I'm sorry we're all out of ballgowns right now," she joked.

"I would *love* to see my dad's face if I come home wearing one of those."

"Let's find something else to make him smile." She threw the clothes over her arm and carried them to an open dressing room, holding the door open for Amanda. "I'll be back to check on you later."

Amanda tried on the first dress and stepped out of the dressing room for an opinion. Sandy was at the register. When she saw Amanda, she shook her head. Amanda went back in for another attempt. She modeled the second dress, and, this time, Sandy nodded in approval. When Gwen finished her fittings, she added her opinion. Sandy offered a few more contenders, until Amanda had tried on all the possibilities. She hadn't expected to enjoy shopping with Gwen, but she had fun and decided on two dresses, three shirts and a pair of designer jeans that hugged her and almost made her look skinny.

Gwen chose the green blouse, but said the floral skirt "wasn't her style." Amanda didn't argue, but she thought it looked pretty. Maybe Gwen ought to consider changing her style.

When they carried their purchases to the register and handed them to Sandy to ring up separately, Amanda noticed a small, carved statue of a Santa Claus on the shelf behind the counter. Maybe it had escaped from the Christmas shop down the street.

"It's summer," Amanda said. "Why do you have a Santa on display?"

Sandy wrapped Amanda's purchases in tissue paper and slid them into a bag. "I like to have symbols of Christmas out all year long. Santa reminds us to be kind and generous with one another. Besides, who wants to be stored away all year and only brought out for one very short month? He'd miss all the fun."

The Santa held a bag of toys and did appear to be having a good time.

"My mom liked Christmas, too, but my dad *really* likes it. You should see our snowmen."

Sandy stopped and stared at her. "Snowmen?"

"Yes, snowmen," Gwen mumbled. "Lots of snowmen. Speaking of your dad, I'd like to go to Wiley's Men's Store next. I think Mac could use some new dress pants."

Sandy dropped Gwen's blouse. "I'm so sorry," she stammered while she refolded the blouse and slid it into a bag. She focused on Amanda and slowly formed a smile. "You have very pretty eyes. They're hazel."

"May we have our bags?" Gwen asked.

Sandy pulled some ribbon from under the counter and tied the handles of the bags with a bow. "Currently, Wiley's has a limited selection of dress pants, but they're having a sale on khakis. Dark taupe is always nice."

Gwen murmured something that sounded vaguely like a "thank you," and turned quickly for the door.

Sandy handed Amanda her bag. "Happy birthday. I hope you enjoy your party this evening and you have a magical fifteenth year."

Amanda felt a tug, a memory of a happy feeling. She wanted to linger in the moment, but Gwen had other plans for her. "Thank you," she said and hurried after Gwen so they could go out and buy fifteen candles.

Chapter Twelve

Bill

How had he let Gwen talk him into this? He wanted to be home, flipping burgers in his own backyard, not sitting on a blanket among a sea of blankets and lawn chairs waiting for the sun to set and the annual fireworks display to begin. Gwen said he'd become too much of a homebody. He agreed, but dragging him here wasn't likely to improve his disposition. It reminded him too much of the Fourth of Julys he'd celebrated with Ellen and Amanda in Lafayette, ones that seemed like a lifetime ago.

"Would you like some fried chicken, Mac?" Gwen had put together a complete picnic, trying to raise Bill's level of enthusiasm.

"You know what I'd like? Lemonade. I saw a sign that said they make it fresh here."

She held up a plastic jug. "I brought iced tea."

Bill stretched his legs, preparing to stand up. His work as a construction foreman sometimes left his joints painful, making him feel like an old man forty years too soon. "I might have some later, but right now, a glass of lemonade is calling me. Would you like me to bring you one?"

She pinched her lips together. "Nelson and Trudy said they'd try to find us." She wanted him to be there so she could introduce him to another set of her friends. He was starting to feel like the fireworks were the warm-up band and he was the main act.

Gwen waved at a friend. Bill had met the friend in a previous outing, but couldn't remember her name. She motioned Gwen over and he took it as his opportunity. "I won't be long," he said.

On his way, he saw Amanda in her new jeans, giggling with her friends as they pretended to ignore a group of boys. She'd be dating soon, too soon for Bill, but, like so many other things in his life, it was out of his control.

As he eyed the lemonade stand, he was distracted again, this time by a stream of brown hair waiting in line for a hot dog. She was wearing a yellow sundress and flat sandals with her long hair in a ponytail. He'd never seen her dressed casually before. She'd always looked professional. Now that he thought of it, he'd never seen her outside of Althea's. It had been months since he'd seen her there, when the force of his desire for her had propelled him out the door. He needed to walk away this time, too, but there he was, taking the position behind her in line. She didn't notice, exhaling loudly and crossing her arms. The line wasn't moving fast enough for her.

"I know," he said. "It's going to take a while."

She turned around, appearing surprised. A few seconds later, she smiled. "You're here."

In the direct beam of the setting sun, her eyes were a lighter shade of brown than he remembered and more vibrant. She seemed younger, too, more likely to enjoy hanging out with Amanda and her friends than with him.

"I haven't seen you since . . ." She let the words drop.

Bill felt exposed, as if someone had written his desire to kiss her that night across his forehead. He wanted to turn and run again, but a man behind him cleared his throat, cueing them it was time for the line to move forward. They closed the gap.

"I haven't been to Althea's for . . ." He thought about it. "A few months. I give the snowmen a rest in summer. I'd hate for them to melt."

"Yes. It's been hot. I had to take the jackets off the Santas." She'd made a joke. He liked this relaxed version of her.

"I'm Sandy," she said. "Sandy Jones."

Now he had a last name to go with the first name. She was whole and complete, and standing in front of him. His stomach felt odd, a queasy feeling he hadn't experienced in years. Some people might call it butterflies. Whatever was happening to him, she was the cause.

"Hello, Sandy Jones. I'm Bill McAllister, but most people call me Mac."

"Bill," she said, nodding her approval. "Mac is nice, but if you don't mind, I'd like to call you Bill."

He laughed. "I haven't been called Bill since middle school, when I decided it was an old man's name—not that Mac isn't—but one of my buddies said it and it stuck. My mother calls me William, even though she knows I hate it, so Bill would be exclusively yours."

She tilted her head, and her eyes seemed to drift over his face. "Exclusively mine. I like it."

Bill knew he should have run while he had the chance. The man behind him cleared his throat again, and Sandy rolled her eyes, a classic Amanda reaction. They all took a giant step forward.

"You know," he said. "I have to tell you, I wouldn't have pegged you as a hot dog person."

"And you would have pegged me correctly. I brought cheese, fruit, and turkey sandwiches on whole wheat, no mayo, thank you, but Virgie wants a hot dog."

"Virgie? Your boyfriend?" *What was he saying? Did he just ask her if she had a boyfriend?* He glanced in the direction of the place where Gwen would be waiting for him. He couldn't see her, but her presence was strong enough that guilt smacked him in the face.

When he looked at Sandy, she was biting her lip. "The boyfriend's name is Trent. Virgie's my grandmother, short for Virginia. We don't believe in titles in my family. Speaking of family, I'm not sure, but I think I met your daughter, Amanda, that is, if you have a daughter. She came into my shop on her birthday."

Bill recalled how excited Amanda had been when she came home from her day with Gwen. She'd modeled all of her clothes and chattered on about the store manager who'd helped her. "You're the one who convinced my daughter to wear a dress again?"

"It's my job to help customers find clothes that make them feel good about themselves."

"How did you know she was my daughter?"

"She said that you like Christmas, and snowmen, and Gwen said . . ." She took a breath. "Anyway, Amanda has your eyes."

Bill could imagine what Gwen had said, but he was glad Sandy had met Gwen, because it made him feel less dishonest. And Sandy had a boyfriend, so they were on even ground.

The line advanced and they both stepped forward to order. "One, please," she said. "No, make it two." She shrugged and glanced back at Bill. "I'm here, so why not?"

"Make it three," Bill said, handing over some cash. "Besides, I haven't had a hot dog since the last time I was at Bobo's, probably a year ago."

She scrunched her nose at the mention of the restaurant.

"Sorry, Bobo's probably isn't to your taste."

"Oh, I've been there, but not since . . ." She seemed to search for a memory, then shook it off. "Bill, I can't let you buy."

"I think I can buy you and Virgie a hot dog, especially since you got my daughter back into a dress."

The vendor handed them the dogs, and they shifted to the condiment table. She added mustard and onions to both of hers, while he dabbed on relish. With their task complete, they stepped away from the table and stood looking at one another.

"Well, Virgie's waiting," she said after a moment, "but before I go, I wanted to let you know that Amanda told me about your wife. I'm so sorry."

Bill was stunned. Amanda rarely talked about the accident, and never to strangers.

Sandy's eyes drifted to his left hand, as if she understood that the absent ring was also still present. "I can't say I understand what you're going through. I don't think it's possible for one person to truly understand another person's pain. I do hope it gets better for you."

He was accustomed to sympathetic words, but Sandy's tenderness seemed to reach inside him. "Some days, it seems better. I stay busy and spend my time trying to keep up with Amanda, but other days . . . it's still tough." He paused. Maybe he'd said too much. He barely knew her, except she felt familiar and safe.

She stared at him for a few long seconds. "I can't imagine losing someone you love so much. Being with Gwen must help."

He thought he heard a question in her words. Now that she put the question out there, he realized he had no answer.

"Speaking of Gwen, I need to get back. She'll be sending out a search party soon." In spite of his words, he was finding it hard to walk away.

"I understand." She wasn't moving either.

The odd sensation in his stomach returned. He felt as if he were back in high school. Maybe both he and Sandy could hang out with Amanda and her friends.

She held up the hotdogs. "Virgie and I thank you for dinner." She lingered for another minute, and then turned her back to him and walked away.

It took all of his willpower not to follow that ponytail and sundress into the crowd. He took some heavy steps and made it back to the blanket and an irritated Gwen.

"You missed Nelson and Trudy," she said. "And where's your lemonade?"

He was still clutching a hotdog. "I got sidetracked. Sorry."

As the fireworks began, Gwen snuggled next to him. Even with her sitting close, he was thinking about big brown eyes somewhere in the crowd watching the same show. Those brown eyes had a boyfriend, and he had his arm around another woman. Neither of those facts could steal the moment.

As the music played in synch with the explosions of color going off above his head, Bill McAllister felt like celebrating.

Chapter Thirteen

Sandy

Elvis Presley's voice vibrated with the words of the song "All Shook Up," which was exactly how Sandy was feeling. She was sitting alone, waiting, simply because a certain man had mentioned the name of the restaurant he had visited a year ago. Until recently, that man had been wearing a wedding ring. He also had a new woman in his life, one that she had met. Still, Sandy couldn't convince herself that the attraction was only hers. Bill might be loyal enough to his relationship to ignore it, but there was something between them. She didn't honestly expect him to walk through the door, but she hadn't seen him since July 4th, nearly a month ago. Since he'd given up his Althea's habit, this place was as close as she could get to him. Pathetic, she knew. She supposed that if she sat alone in Bobo's listening to doowop music long enough, she'd eventually get over him.

Bobo's was as she remembered it—fake vintage with red vinyl seats and chrome tables. The walls were decorated with black and white photos of carhops mixed with James Dean types leaning up against their hotrods. It was the local tribute to a fifties diner with the classic American fare of hamburgers, hot dogs, French fries, shakes and a dessert favorite—apple pie ala mode.

Trent had brought her here on one of their first dates. The fall day had been brisk, and the place warm and inviting. Their relationship was new and exciting with all the possibilities ahead of them.

She had come here today thinking of Bill, but Trent had once again inserted into her thoughts, just as he had done when Bill had said the name of the restaurant. This place reminded her that her relationship with Trent was still unresolved. For the last few weeks, she had tried to return her attention to him. Neither had volunteered information about the evening they'd spent apart, but Sandy assumed he had been enjoying barbecue with a certain co-worker named Frankie. Both Sandy and Trent had seemed content to continue with their routines, except their conversations now had silences that neither seemed able to fill. Her feelings for Trent bounced from guilt to frustration to anger to sadness.

She was definitely feeling all shook up.

A man climbed out from a booth near here and dropped some money into the jukebox. By the gray in his hair and the lines on his forehead, Sandy put him at about seventy. The song, "I Only Have Eyes for You," played and he shuffled his feet in a dance movement, focusing his attention on the booth. A woman of similar vintage, his wife if Sandy were to guess, smiled and shook her head. He danced his way toward her, and Sandy assumed they were now looking into each other's eyes, to the exclusion of all others. She sighed, wondering whose eyes might be gazing at her at seventy and if he'd still have a dance left for her.

The young waitress dressed in jeans rolled up at the ankle, bobby socks, and saddle oxfords, delivered a comforting hot chocolate with extra whipped cream and chocolate sprinkles.

The waitress stepped away and behind her, a teenage boy appeared. He wore a blue Captain America t-shirt, khaki cargo shorts, a baseball hat turned backwards and bright green Vans tennis shoes. Sandy liked his style.

"Hey there," he said. "Remember me?"

She laughed. "I do remember you."

A couple of weeks ago, he'd come into Ginger's, asking for the manager, his claim that he was searching for a present for his mother. She'd shown him a few blouses, but when she saw his grimace at the price tags, she'd redirected him.

"How did the socks work out?" she asked.

He lowered his eyes, confirming her suspicion that the gift likely had another recipient. "Not bad. Not bad," he said.

"Are you having dinner here?"

"It's Dad's night to cook, so we're doing take out. He called in an order. Usually he barbecues, but we were out of propane." His voice cracked slightly, and he flinched a little with embarrassment. "Dad wanted to switch their cooking nights, but Mom had her feet up. You know how girls are."

She laughed again. "I do."

He scratched his chin, perhaps hoping for a whisker. "You waiting for a boyfriend or something?"

After the time she had spent with him in her store trying to decide on the perfect pair of socks, which turned out to be a soft grey cashmere at her suggestion, she had become accustomed to his personal questions. *Did you go to school here? What's your favorite color? Favorite food? Any kids? Pets?*

For his latest question, she had no answer.

"Chip," the boy's father called. "Quit charming the ladies and let's go." He held up two bags of food. A grease stain was already darkening the bottom of the bag.

"Guess I'd better go. Dad has finished his cooking. See ya later."

"Sure. Come to the shop anytime. It's never too early to shop for Christmas."

His dad handed him one of the bags of food and slapped him lightly on the back. As they walked out, Sandy realized how ridiculous she must appear, sitting alone, waiting for someone who didn't even know she was here. She took a quick sip of her hot chocolate, put some cash on the table, and prepared to leave.

The door swung open.

In a town the size of St. Clair, there was a high probability she would see someone she knew. A friend from high school. One of Virgie's cronies. Even a young customer from Ginger's. It was also possible that Bill might walk through that door. The one she didn't expect to see was her boyfriend, laughing as he trailed after a young woman with shoulder length blonde hair. The woman was tall and slender, her physique mirroring Trent's. Sandy might have thought they made a nice couple, if the second half of the duo wasn't already part of a couple.

Trent saw her and the smile slid off his face. His partner continued walking.

"Hello," Sandy said, pasting on a smile.

"Sandy? What are you doing here?"

What was she doing here, indeed? She considered the obvious ploy of answering his question with the same question, but instead, pointed to her cup.

"Hot chocolate?" His eyes narrowed. "It's eighty degrees outside."

A sarcastic comeback pinged in her head. *Thanks for the weather report.* She was grateful Virgie had trained her in the art of editing, which had saved her from numerous arguments with Trent.

His companion noticed he had stopped and returned to his side.

She was pretty, but her eyebrows would have benefitted from some shaping, and she definitely needed a different color shirt. The yellow cotton button-up washed out her features. If she were in her store, Sandy would have suggested royal blue or a nice cranberry. Sandy wished she could laugh at herself for contemplating a makeover on the girl currently out with her boyfriend.

Trent now had two pairs of eyes on him. He shifted uncomfortably. "Sandy, this is Frankie . . . Francesca."

Frankie-Francesca offered a fleeting, "Hello," but her gape lasted longer, either completing a makeover of Sandy in her mind or simply sizing her up.

"We worked late," Trent interjected. "We're just getting some pie." He had donned another new shirt, this one a light-blue poly-cotton blend that was perfect for a warm summer night—an eighty degree summer night as she'd been informed. Sandy decided she missed his t-shirts with the computer code gibberish that she could never decode. At least she understood that version of Trent. "You can join us," he offered.

"No, thank you. I don't want to interrupt."

"You wouldn't be interrupting," Frankie said, offering the courtesy to try to cover Trent's forced invitation. "I'll get a table," she said, and headed toward the back of the restaurant.

When she was out of range, Trent said, "Did you know I'd be here?"

"How would I know that? You haven't brought me here since the first month we were dating."

The reality of it struck her. This place that was something old was where Trent started something new.

"I don't know," he said. "It seems strange that you're here."

Sandy considered all the events over the last few weeks and had to agree; it was all very strange. She couldn't begin to say what was in Bill's heart, or even in her own, but she hadn't been ready to dispose of the life she had with Trent. She hadn't honestly believed that Trent was ready to dispose of her.

He folded his arms. "Don't get all crazy about this."

She crossed hers in return. "Is there any reason I should?"

He hesitated and shot a glance at the booth where Frankie was waiting for him, only for a few seconds, but it was enough.

Ironically, the jukebox flipped to a new song, "The Great Pretender." Before seeing Trent with Frankie, Sandy assumed she had been the only one pretending. Now she could see they both were. Even more devastating was the mirror Trent had held up for her to see. She'd been deceiving him, and herself. She couldn't live in one life while hoping for another.

She stood up. "I'm leaving now." She tried to step around Trent, but he touched her arm to stop her.

"Do you even care?"

She might have said, "Of course, I care," if not for the older couple who had seemed so in love walking past them hand in hand on their way out. She wanted to be that couple, the ones that shared the kind of love that endured for decades. At one time, she imagined that Trent might be that other half. Now, that thought seemed far away.

"I can't talk about this here, Trent. Enjoy your . . . pie."

She stepped around him and concentrated on putting one foot ahead of the other to get to out the door. She didn't look back.

Chapter Fourteen

Amanda

Amanda stared at her pink wall. She'd outgrown the pink, but hadn't been ready to change it. She and her mother had painted it themselves right after they moved in. She wished she would have gone for blue or green, some color that didn't scream little girl. She could have kept those colors forever, never having to paint over their shared project and the memories of that day. She could still see her mom with a paintbrush in hand standing on the stepstool when her dad came home. When he'd seen the color, he'd squinted as if in pain.

"Our baby girl wanted pink," her mom had said.

"And whatever our baby girl wants . . ." he had replied, repeating one of their familiar sayings.

"Our baby girl gets." She'd stepped down and held out the brush. "Amanda and I were just talking about taking a break." They hadn't been. "And you're so good with your hands."

He'd accepted the brush. "Okay, Tom Sawyer, I'll finish up, but only under protest and the promise of something sweet."

"We'll see. Amanda and I will be back in later to check on your work. Don't disappoint us." When the two of them made it to the hallway, they'd both broken into giggles.

"I heard that," he'd said from the bedroom, and they'd laughed harder.

She missed the laughter, but the laughter wasn't mixed into the color of the wall. She could change it. She closed her eyes and imagined the room in baby blue, sage green or purple. Her dad would have a fit if she asked for purple. When she opened her eyes, the room was still pink. As much as she wanted a more adult color, she was having a hard time letting go. But change was going to happen, whether she was ready for it or not.

Amanda had been thinking about how much her life had changed since the night her mother died. Their house seemed empty. Sometimes when Gwen was there, it felt more like the way it had been before, but then it always went back to empty. Amanda didn't want Gwen to move in or anything, but it was nice to not always have the sadness hanging over them. Amanda probably didn't have to worry about Gwen moving in, since she hadn't seen her for weeks. Her dad wasn't talking, but Amanda guessed it had something to do with Sandy, the manager from Ginger's.

On the Fourth of July, Amanda had seen Sandy standing in line for hot dogs and was thinking about going over to say hello, when she saw her dad step into the line behind her. A coincidence, she thought, until Sandy turned and they appeared to know one another, not as if they'd just met, but like they *knew* one another. Amanda hated to gawk, but they were standing close—definitely close—and they were staring at one another, as if no one else was there. If the man standing behind her dad hadn't nudged them, they wouldn't have moved at all.

Her mom and dad used to be that way sometimes. Other people could be talking all around them, but they'd only pay attention to each other. Amanda asked her mom once why they spent so much time together when there were other people around. She'd replied, "Who do you like to spend your time with?"

Amanda thought about it. "Monica, but she's my best friend."

"Dad is my best friend."

Amanda couldn't understand it at the time. She'd never thought about them being friends, only parents. Sandy and her dad might be friends—or something more. Maybe they had that funny feeling that couples get. She understood. Her funny feeling was over a boy named Chip Dugan.

When she first moved to St. Clair, she'd had to start her new school mid-term. The principal had interrupted the class and introduced her to all those unfamiliar eyes that seemed to be judging her, but then a voice came from the back of the room.

"McAllister, huh? Got an empty seat over here if you're brave enough." She'd followed the voice to a smallish student who appeared to have wandered into the wrong classroom. The kids laughed, but the principal didn't.

"Ah, yes, Mr. Dugan. Amanda, if you've brought some bravery with you, please take the seat next to Charles—"

"Chip," the voice piped in. "Charles is my father and I'm way better looking." All the kids laughed again.

This time, the principal almost smiled. "Take the seat next to Charles Dugan's son, and good luck."

She'd made it down the aisle and fell into the seat, hoping to become instantly invisible, willing her blushing cheeks to return to some shade of normal.

Chip leaned over and whispered, "Don't worry, McAllister. I've got you covered."

He'd been calling her "McAllister" ever since. She liked it—and him.

After her mom died, he'd made it his personal mission to make her laugh. He'd say, "Chip Dugan, Court Jester, at your service," and then he'd do some crazy moves with his arms and legs until she laughed and begged him to stop.

When she told him about seeing Sandy with her dad, he said he'd set up surveillance on the "broad," using a voice that sounded like an old-time detective. She imagined him across the street from Ginger's on his bicycle with binoculars. She thought he was joking until he said he'd gone undercover, playing a customer searching for a present for his mother.

"What did you think of her?" she'd asked.

He'd proceeded to list all the details he had gathered while she helped him search for a present. She had graduated from St. Clair High. Her favorite color was red and sometimes green, except in the spring when she liked yellow. Her favorite food was ice cream—pralines and cream in the summer and chocolate chip in the winter. She'd worked at Ginger's for five years and had been the manager for three. Her favorite musical instrument was the piano. She'd taken lessons as kid, but she didn't play anymore. Chip suggested the tuba as a new favorite, since he'd chosen it as his instrument for the school band. He'd said if his mom was going to make him participate in the marching band, he was going to make it count. He'd ended his report with, "She's nice. She's going to rank low on the wicked stepmother scale."

"So I won't get to play Cinderella."

"Too bad. I think I'd make a cool Prince Charming."

She'd blushed when he said it, because she'd started to think of him as her Prince Charming. They'd always been friends, but a few weeks ago, when they were alone, he kissed her lightly on the side of her mouth. He hadn't missed her lips. He just decided that was where he wanted the kiss to be.

Remembering that moment, she reached up and lightly touched the spot where he had kissed her. As she did, her cell phone rang announcing Chip as the caller. She blushed again.

"Bobo's!" Chip said, before she even had a chance to say hello.

"What do you mean, Bobo's?"

"She was at Bobo's tonight. Alone!"

"Who was?"

"Sandy. Your Dad's squeeze. Keep up, McAllister."

She still liked it when he called her by her last name. "I didn't say Sandy was his squeeze. I only said they stood close together at the Fourth of July picnic."

"And you said they stared at each other. I'm telling you, guys don't stare at girls unless they like them."

"He could like her, but he wasn't with her tonight. It's Wednesday. " She thought of him sitting by her mother's grave, the place she knew he would be. "He wouldn't be meeting Sandy."

"But she was waiting for someone. Why else would you sit alone at a restaurant? And she wasn't even having dinner. Mighty suspicious if you ask me. I think we should up our surveillance."

"Or I could just ask my dad."

"He'll never break. I've seen his type before." The old-time detective voice was back. "I'll call you tomorrow and we'll plan our stakeout."

Planning a stakeout with Chip did sound like more fun than talking to her dad about a woman. "Okay, Detective Dugan, call me tomorrow."

After they hung up, Amanda opened her chest of drawers and pulled out the pair of light grey cashmere socks Chip had purchased on his undercover mission. They were the first present a boy had ever given her and the softest pair of socks she had ever owned.

She held them next to her pink wall. They were a pretty color—very grownup. "What do you think, Mom?" She waited, wishing the silence could answer her.

She looked around the room and landed on a photo of herself at five years old. She was on a swing with her mom in the background. Amanda wished she could remember the day. Her dad had snapped the picture when she was in flight. Her mom had her arms extended, pushing her upward. They were both laughing.

"I'll take that as a *yes*," Amanda said to the photo.

Tomorrow, she'd tell her dad they would need to go out and buy some light grey paint.

Chapter Fifteen

Bill

Bill brushed aside some leaves that had blown off the maple tree next to the path. He laid a bouquet of daisies on the grass, knowing the delicate flowers wouldn't last in the heat, but they'd been her favorite. His hand trembled. Ellen was here, in a place she should not have been.

Across the grounds, a tent flapping in the wind stood ready for a service in the morning. He could almost see the line of cars with their headlights on, the occupants following each other prepared to share their grief. He closed his eyes to chase away the image. He'd come to talk to Ellen. Sometimes on weekends, Amanda would join him, but Wednesday nights were his alone.

He followed the engraved letters of her name and spoke to her softly. "Hey, Ellen. It's me. Wednesday again." He tried to imagine what she would say. She wouldn't be happy he was here. She'd probably say something like, "Yes, Mac. It's Wednesday. Now why aren't you out doing something fun?" Fun? He couldn't imagine what that might be. He was here and Ellen was just going to have to listen to him.

"Sometimes the weeks fly by. Other times, they seem like they'll never end. Today was a rough one. I did a final walk-through with a young couple on that two-story model, the one with the deck outside the master bedroom. You remember that one. I showed you the plans. They were so excited, so much like us when we started out. They were expecting their first child, and to have a new home . . . it was perfect. Maybe too perfect. I don't know why it's sometimes so hard to see other people being happy. We had our time. I just didn't expect it to end so soon."

He rubbed his forehead. The lines there seemed to get deeper every day. He straightened the pinwheel that Amanda had "planted" there.

"Remember when you planted that pinwheel garden for Amanda?" he asked.

Years ago—another lifetime—Amanda had placed a pinwheel in their garden so it could grow like another one of the flowers. The next day, Ellen planted one next to it, and added a new one every day until the garden had sprouted a dozen pinwheels. "I *knew* they would grow!" Amanda had said. This tribute was one simple way Amanda was able to remember her mother without carrying any of the bitterness that he was fighting to overcome. "She's growing up, Ellen. I can't seem to stop her."

He searched his brain for something else to say, something that would keep him here with her. He was finding it more difficult to continue his conversations. He wanted to keep his focus on Ellen, on her laugh, her blonde hair, her blue eyes. Another picture kept breaking through. He imagined brown eyes across town, maybe picking up another Santa at Althea's. In ten minutes, he could be there.

He couldn't convince himself to make that trip. Sandy had probably given up on him anyway. He looked upward, following the movement of the fast moving clouds. *Keep moving, Mac. Is that what Ellen would tell him?*

"I love you, honey. See you next week."

He trudged past the stone angel in the middle of the grounds on the way back to his truck. It might have been a beautiful statue if he didn't hate the reason he had to see it. He climbed into his truck and drove to The Rusty Nail as he did every Wednesday where he'd have a beer at the bar. The rest of the week belonged to other people, but this was his time.

The bartender, Candace, was in her spot, pulling on the tap. She saw Bill and motioned with her chin to a booth. He turned his head to see an unsmiling Gwen. He'd pulled back from their relationship, one of the many things he had chosen to avoid. By coming here, she was telling him avoidance time was about to end. Candace met his gaze and nodded with encouragement. He had to say, she was good at reading people.

He slid into the plastic seat of the booth across from Gwen, the squeak causing him to flinch. She was wearing a shiny green blouse that accented the color of her eyes. The last time she wore it, he'd told her she looked pretty. He didn't think a compliment would help his position tonight.

"Hey," he said, trying to sound pleased, "this is a surprise."

"If the mountain won't come to Muhammad, then Muhammad must come to the mountain."

"I guess I'm the mountain?"

"You're immovable enough." She glanced around, her frown deepening. "You like this place?"

He'd never thought about whether he liked it. It had simply become the stop on his way home. He followed her critical eye to the chalkboard that listed the weekly events—country-line dancing lessons on Tuesday and bands on Thursday, Friday, and Saturday. Wednesdays were quiet, which was the reason he'd been able to continue his weekly ritual.

Candace delivered a beer he hadn't ordered yet. She narrowed her eyes at Gwen. "Anything else you need, Mac?"

"No, thanks, Candace."

"If I'd ever been invited here," Gwen huffed, "I might be on a first name basis with the waitress, too."

"I'm the *bartender* and part owner," Candace said, "but you may call me Ms. Silva."

"All right, Ms. Silva, would you bartend me another martini?"

Candace winked, as if to say *touché*. She left them to their conversation.

Bill folded his arms and leaned back against the booth, putting as much distance as he could between them. "Go ahead. The mountain is listening."

Gwen leaned forward. "How long are you going to do this?"

"Do what?"

"You know what. Hide out in the garage. Avoid me. Stay stuck in this weekly habit." She hesitated, as if deciding whether to press on. She let the words tumble out. "I can't compete with a memory. No one can."

"You're not competing, Gwen. We talked about this when we first started seeing one another. I told you I was still struggling with my wife's death. I know you think I should be over it –"

"No, what I think is that you don't *want* to be over it. Life keeps going, Mac, whether you like it or not. You have a daughter who needs you and we could all have a life together, but you keep pushing me away. We talked about moving in together."

Actually, *she'd* talked about it, while he had remained fiercely ambiguous in his responses.

"I'm not ready for that kind of commitment." He glanced at the bar, where Candace seemed to be watching him with a level of concern he wouldn't have expected. She had somehow involved herself in the drama. Normally, he liked his privacy, but right now, he didn't mind the show of support. "I'll get your drink for you. I think *Ms. Silva* doesn't want to be accused of being a waitress again."

At the bar, Candace slid the drink toward him and whispered, "I made it a double."

Bill smiled and headed back to Gwen, whose frown now resembled a scowl. *And I thought Muhammad was a pacifist.* He set the drink in front of her and sat down, taking a couple of swigs of beer before going back in for another round. "Why tonight? We had plans to see each other this weekend. Couldn't we have talked then?"

"You've been distracted. I wanted to capture your attention." She took a sip of her drink, and then another. "The waitress makes a good martini."

He couldn't deny he'd been distracted, but he'd hoped that, with time, he could work through his feelings for Sandy and get back to place where he was in charge of his emotions. "You know I'm grateful to you, Gwen. You pulled me out of a dark spot last year."

"Grateful?" The word stung her in a way he hadn't intended. "I don't want you to be grateful, and I might have pulled you out, but you're sliding back in. I don't think I'm strong enough to heave dead weight." She winced. "Sorry. Sometimes my mouth says things before I can stop it."

"It's okay. You're right. It's how I feel."

"The thing is, Mac, I want to get married again. I figure my first marriage was a trial run. I think I'd be good at it now."

"Gwen, I . . ."

She held up her hand. "I'll cue you when it's your turn to speak."

Despite the serious conversation, he smiled.

"Forty is looming and, yes, I know age doesn't *loom* for men. I think the only way to get those numbers to stop staring at me is to make my life into what I want it to be." She tipped her glass and finished the drink. "I want to have a nice house and a yard so I can plant an herb garden. I'm thinking about getting a dog. You know the kind, with the wirey hair and long face. What are they called?"

"I can speak?"

"Just on the dog topic."

"I believe they're fox terriers."

"Yes, one of those. I want a dog and I want a partner, not necessarily in that order. I want someone who believes I might just be the best thing ever. I never expected that kind of affection from you, but I realize I *should* expect it. Today, I received a wedding invitation from Nelson and Trudy—the couple you *didn't* meet on the Fourth of July when you got mysteriously sidetracked."

She couldn't have known just how sidetracked he had been—and still was.

"It's the third marriage for Nelson and the second for Trudy. Their kids are almost grown and there's no reason for them to get married, except they want to be together." She glanced at her empty glass and then at the bar. He guessed she was willing it to refill itself. "I want to be with someone who wants to be together for no other reason than we care about each other." She leaned back in the booth. "Okay, now you can speak."

She was wrong. He was speechless. "I . . ."

"So far so good."

He wanted to be honest with her. "Right now, I can't even think about marriage. Sometimes I find it difficult to put my boots on in the morning."

"So how about in a year? Think those boots will be easier to put on?"

He ran his fingers through his hair. "God, Gwen, I don't know."

"Okay, try this one. You're sitting on your bed, trying to put on your boots. Am I the one beside you?"

Bill rubbed his chin. He'd forgotten to shave that morning. If Gwen had been there, she would have reminded him. She would keep their lives in order. But in the picture Gwen was presenting, the only person he could see beside him was Sandy, a woman whose hand he had yet to hold. He realized he was doing it again, sitting here with Gwen and thinking about Sandy.

Candace delivered another beer to him. He hadn't ordered it, but he didn't mind having it. "How about you, Sunshine?" she said to Gwen. "Anything else to drink?"

"Nope. I think I'm done." She waited until Candace left before she spoke. "I'm going to make this easy on you. Brett Tucker invited me—actually, he invited *us*—to his built-in barbecue warming party. What kind of man hosts a party just to celebrate building a barbecue? Anyway, he invited me, but he said I should bring you along. Brett always liked me in school. I liked him, too, and now that he's divorced . . ." She shrugged. "I don't know, but I like the way he looks at me."

Bill could understand. Sandy could make his heart beat faster just by smiling at him. "I met him on Fourth of July, right?"

"He was the one with the big chin. He has the shoulders to match, so I guess it all works."

She was letting him off easy, and again he was grateful to her. "When we first started going out," he said, "I didn't have any expectations."

"Maybe that's the problem. You never *expected* anything. You never wanted anything. I want to be angry with you, but you're too sad for me to be angry. Your life will never be as it was, but it can be good again. Life goes on, Mac, if you let it. I wish you would have dumped me, so I could yell at you."

"You can still yell at me."

"You're not much of a sparring partner. If you had the energy, or the desire, to fight back, then I think we might have a chance. As it is, I don't think we have much of anything at all."

He wanted to say something that would smooth the rough edges and spin the ending into something positive, but all he could manage was, "I'm sorry."

"Yeah, me too. Tell Amanda . . ." She rubbed her temples, the strain showing. "Never mind. I'll talk to her myself."

He was hurting a woman who'd been kind to him—one he cared about. Now Amanda would have another change in her life over which she had no control. He'd have a few things to say to Ellen next week.

Chapter Sixteen

Amanda

Amanda parked her bike outside Ginger's and peered past the mannequins in the window. She could pretend she was shopping for a back-to-school wardrobe, but if Sandy were there, she'd find her something that fit perfectly and Amanda would want to buy it. She had a little cash with her, but probably not enough. She could try the Chip method of shopping for socks, except going home with an article of clothing really wasn't her goal. She didn't exactly know her goal, but her bike had insisted she come here, so here they were.

Chip would be disappointed if he knew she'd come on her own. Their "stakeouts" had been limited to him riding by on his bicycle when he wasn't taking care of his little brother. He said his mom was cramping his style with the babysitting gig, but when she'd offered payment, he'd decided he could put his detective career temporarily on hold.

Sandy stepped out of the store wearing a dark green dress that flared at the bottom and hit a couple of inches above her knees. She looked cute. And young.

Sandy walked toward her. "Amanda?"

Amanda dug her hands into the pockets of her shorts. "Hi." She wished she'd prepared something to say.

"Are you coming in?"

"No. Just looking."

"I see." Sandy tilted her head. "I was going to lunch. Would you like to join me?"

"No." She didn't mean to sound rude. "Thank you."

Sandy continued to study her. "How did the outfits work out?"

"Fine." Okay. Now it was awkward. What was the matter with her? She should be able to say what was on her mind, except she didn't quite know. She only knew that her bike wanted to come here and say something important. Stupid bike.

"I'm glad you came back," Sandy said, ignoring Amanda's obvious lack of communication skills. "I realized as you were leaving on your birthday that I probably knew your father. I saw him on Fourth of July and he confirmed it. I'd say 'small world,' but I've never liked that saying."

"Me neither." She was still having problems with the words, but she was starting to relax. She had wondered if Sandy would talk about her dad, or if maybe it was a secret. Amanda still hadn't asked him about her. "I saw you with my dad at the picnic. I was going to come over and say hi to you, but then you started talking to him, and you were both smiling and standing close."

"So you thought . . . no, we've only spoken a few times. We're more acquaintances than friends, and I know he's seeing Gwen."

"They broke up." Amanda blurted it out before she had a chance to think how it might sound, but she really did want Sandy to know. Maybe her bike wasn't so stupid.

She hesitated. "I'm sorry. Are you okay?"

Sandy never said what Amanda thought she was going to say. After her mom died, everyone asked if she was okay. When her dad and Gwen broke up, no one seemed to think it affected her. Sometimes Gwen made her crazy, but she liked the way she made them dinner and brought desserts, and she especially liked the way she made her dad laugh, at least at the beginning. Not much made him laugh these days.

"Yeah. I kind of miss her, but I guess I'm okay." Amanda paused. "How *old* are you?" She was being rude again, but she felt she *had* to know. She told Chip he should have asked. He'd offered to make a return visit, but she'd said Sandy would think he was stalking her.

"I'm thirty-one."

"You look younger."

She smiled. "My junior department dress is throwing you off."

"You shop in the junior department?"

She shrugged. "I like clothes. I shop in *every* department. Some days, when I'm wearing suits, I look quite old."

"I don't think so. You wore a suit the day I met you, and you still looked young and you wear your hair long, like my friends." Amanda self-consciously touched the strands of her fine, dark-blonde hair. Sandy's hair fell halfway down her back and it was the color of Hershey bar. She'd trade her in a second.

"Trent likes it longer," Sandy said. "So do I, I suppose."

"Who's Trent?"

She pushed out a breath. "He is . . . *was* my boyfriend. We broke up."

"You broke up, too?" Amanda's thoughts buzzed. "Why?"

Sandy blinked, and Amanda could see the gears turning. "The easy answer is that he likes someone else, but I think it's because we didn't care enough about each other to stay together."

"Like Dad and Gwen?"

She blinked again. "I don't really know them. I only know Gwen as a customer and your dad from Althea's. It seems your dad and I both like to shop for Christmas—all year long. A little crazy, I know. I haven't seen him there in months, so I guess I'm the only crazy one left."

"No. He's still crazy, just a different kind." He seemed sad all the time, except when she saw him at the picnic with Sandy, he'd looked happy. "Can you talk to him?" Amanda wasn't trying to set up her dad on a date, well, not exactly, but she had to do *something*. Otherwise, he might just stay the way he was, which wasn't good for him, or her. She tried kicking him back to Althea's, but he refused, saying he had enough snowmen. Her old dad would never say they had enough snowmen. Amanda definitely had to act.

"We all have to grieve in our own way, Amanda," Sandy said gently. "He misses your mom. I know you do, too."

"I do, but. . ." She almost hated to say it, because it sounded like she wasn't sad anymore, and she was, sometimes, but not every minute of the day. "Sometimes, I have dreams about her. They seem so real. She walks in the door, and I feel like I can reach out and touch her. We both know she's gone and it's okay. She's happy. I wish my dad would have that dream so he would feel better."

"He will, when he's ready." She took a step toward Amanda. "You know, I dream about my father."

"Is he . . . dead?"

"No, at least I don't think so. I've never met him."

"You never met him? How can you dream about someone you've never met?"

"Silly, huh? Sometimes he's wearing swim trunks, and the other night, he was in a pin-stripe suit, sitting at my dinner table talking to James Bond."

"You watch Bond movies?" She seemed too sophisticated to watch the action movies Amanda's dad liked. "And he was in your dream?"

"Yes, I'm a 007 fan, but don't tell Trent." She pushed her hair behind her ear. "I guess it doesn't matter now." She glanced down the street.

Amanda tried to see where she was looking, but it just looked like a bunch of stores to her.

"I have an idea," Sandy said. "Why don't we give your dad a present? Maybe that will make him feel better."

"What kind of present?"

"I know just the thing. Can you come by tomorrow?"

Amanda didn't see how a new shirt or a pair of socks would make him feel better, but she was willing to try. "My bike might be going in this direction tomorrow."

"Good. Are you sure you can't join me for lunch?"

"Are you going to Bobo's?"

Sandy tilted her head again and Amanda could see the question in her eyes.

"Chip says you like it there."

"Chip?"

"Chip Dugan." Amanda lowered her eyes.

Sandy didn't respond, likely waiting for Amanda to explain how the boy who shopped for socks knew who she was and had relayed information back to Amanda.

"He's a friend of mine," Amanda said quietly. She assumed the guilt had written itself on her face.

"I remember Chip. The inquisitive boy. And he's your friend."

"Yes. He...we...well, Dad needed...you know." She'd lost her words again.

"I'm not sure I do know, but I enjoyed meeting Chip. He's unique and interesting and quite a gentleman. Don't you think so?"

She shrugged. "He's nice."

"Very nice. No Bobo's today, but I'm going to The Cheese Pantry. They have good salads *and* soft serve ice cream."

The Cheese Pantry. Amanda's mom had taken her there for lunch . . . and ice cream cones. She remembered sitting at the counter and spinning on the barstool. At the time, she knew she was too old for it, but then her mom spun hers, too, and they both laughed like two best friends.

"I think my mom would have liked you," Amanda said.

Sandy smiled slowly. "I think I would have liked her, too."

Amanda had that odd sensation again—a memory of being happy and loved. She'd felt it when she lit fourteen candles for the important people in her life. The first candle was for her mom. She also lit candles for her dad, her grandparents, some teachers, her close friends, Chip (although she didn't tell him), and even Gwen. She seemed to be holding her last candle for a specific person, one she couldn't name at the time. Maybe it was for Sandy.

Sandy motioned her forward. "Come on—ice cream awaits."

Chapter Seventeen

Sandy

Sandy loved her grandmother's house, the place where she'd spent so much time as a child. She loved the spiral staircase, the thick birch floors, and the old stone fireplace with the river rocks darkened from years of use. She loved her tiny room, nestled in the back of the second floor. Typically, on a summer night, she'd be sitting on the front porch swing sipping the flavored ice tea that Virgie had made for her. Tonight she was in her old room, sitting on the twin bed of her childhood. Thinking.

On Tuesdays, for past two years, Trent would pickup groceries on the way to her house. Sandy would arrive home and pause in the doorway to listen for the sounds of NPR playing on the radio and Trent's steady chop of salad against the cutting board. She would walk through the door, kiss him, and go upstairs to change for their evening of dinner and TV that would likely include an episode of Nova.

She hadn't realized how those evenings had become such an important part of her life and how much she missed them. More than anything, she missed being a couple. Trent had filled a space in her life that was now empty. Her heart was starting to heal, but Tuesday nights were a void she hadn't yet filled, and so she was here. Thinking.

"Virgie says you've been up here for an hour." Candace stood in the doorway, her hand propped on her hip, wearing a jumpsuit with yellow and pink metallic polka dots. Either she'd been transported back in time or she was on her way to a disco.

"What are you wearing?"

"We're mixing it up at the bar. Tonight is 70s night. What are you doing up here anyway?"

"Thinking."

"That's never good. Why don't you come to the Rusty Nail? A little Saturday Night Fever might be what you need, even on a Tuesday. You can bring that stuffed shirt you call a boyfriend. Maybe we can loosen him up a little."

"I think he's loose enough. You could invite him and Frankie. She looks like she can handle the Hustle." Just because her heart was healing didn't mean she couldn't be a little bitter.

"Oh, Sandy." She stepped into the room and fell onto the dorm room sized futon Sandy had insisted on having when she was in high school. Candace frowned and squirmed into it. "Can't we get rid of this torture device?"

"Where would you sit?"

"In the living room!" She laughed, but then made an effort to be serious. "I am sorry about Trent."

"You never liked him anyway."

Candace didn't deny it. "He was nice enough." By her standards, she was being generous, in the same way people speak kindly of the dearly departed. He *was* nice enough, and he had cared about Sandy. Until he didn't. If she were being honest, his distraction coincided with her own, and if they needed to assign blame, there might be some jostling for first in line. Candace preferred to designate men as the Root of All Evil, conveniently forgetting who offered whom the Apple. "However," Candace said, "I might have to celebrate that I won't have to call you Mrs.—what was that horrible last name of his?"

"Lankershim."

Candace tried to bite back her laugh, but it burst through. "Maybe the women in this house are better off without men."

"Virgie had a good marriage," Sandy reminded her.

"To Art, but you never met the disaster who was my father."

"Virgie said he wanted to be a good man. He just didn't know how."

"Oh, he knew how. Just not with us. He had another family, remember?" Pain flashed in Candace's eyes.

Occasionally, Sandy saw a glimpse of the feelings Candace kept locked away, like sneaking a peak at the first page of a diary. Candace's father left when she was eight years old. He told Virgie that his Portuguese roots were calling him home, not to Portugal, but to Newark to a woman he knew before he married Virgie. He moved in with her and her four children, leaving his Indiana family in a trail of dust, checking in at first on holidays, and then nothing at all. "Virgie sees the best in people," Candace said. "Like you. I guess I'm the only who didn't get rose-colored lenses in my glasses."

Sandy shifted uncomfortably on her bed. Candace was right about the living room being a better location for conversation, but she was grateful for the privacy. "Speaking of fathers . . ."

Candace cut her off. "I thought we were talking about two-timing boyfriends."

"Trent wasn't two-timing," Sandy insisted. "He was simply interested in pursuing another relationship."

"You must have just polished your glasses." She shook her head. "How can you possibly be my daughter?"

"I don't know. I wasn't there, but speaking of someone who was . . . I found my father."

"Was he lost?"

"You said you didn't where he was."

"I think I said I didn't *care* where he was."

"Well, I do. And I found him."

"You're talking about Sander?"

"Who else?" Sandy hated it when her mother tried to bury the topic of her father. She'd been successful for years, but Sandy wasn't going to be put off any longer. "Sander Jones, whose real name is Elliott, who now lives in San Diego. My father."

She laughed. "Oh yes, *Elliott*."

"You forgot his real name?"

She shrugged. "Of course not, but everyone called him Sander."

"Don't you want to ask how I found him?"

"The better question is *why*. Do you need a surf lesson? We were only together for a year. I don't know why you're so focused on him."

"It's seems perfectly natural for me to focus on my *father*." Since she already opened the can, she decided there was room for a few more worms. "A couple of things have been bothering me."

Candace eyed the doorway, but one uncomfortable futon made a quick escape challenging. She heaved a sigh. "Okay, hit me."

"You never told me he gave me money. I thought it came from Art and Virgie."

She glanced at the doorway again. "I never said it was from Art and Virgie. The money was there to help you. And it did. Can't you let it go?"

"And I have my house because of it. Shouldn't I be able to thank him, or at least ask him why he went to so much trouble if he wasn't going to be part of my life? But you already know the reason, don't you?"

"Sandy. . ." Her brown eyes, similar to Sandy's but darker and more compelling, were asking her to stop. She couldn't stop. She'd come too far.

"When I was young," Sandy said, "you told me stories about the happy times you had living in that tiny cottage with Sander near the beach. You gave me shells you collected there and pieces of sea glass. One time you told me my father held me in his arms and said he couldn't believe he had such a beautiful child, but when I asked why we couldn't go visit, you said he couldn't see us anymore. Which version was true?"

"Both." Pain flashed in her eyes again, and Sandy knew she'd caught a glimpse of the second page of the diary. "It was a long time ago."

"Thirty-one years, I know." For a woman wearing a disco outfit popular over forty years ago, her mother was remarkably afraid of looking at the past. "He has his own life," Candace continued. "He doesn't need someone popping in unannounced turning everything upside down."

"I'm his daughter. I should be able to pop in unannounced. Maybe he deserves to have everything turned upside down. He should want to know me."

"I thought you would have outgrown this by now. You can't get back all those years and suddenly have a relationship. It's too late for him to take you to the father-daughter dance. I don't want you to be hurt."

"The way you were."

"Yes, the way I was. Let it go, Sandy."

"It's my choice," she said with more bravado than she felt. "You don't have to protect me anymore."

"Like it or not, I'll always protect you."

Sandy nodded in a way that said she understood. Not that it mattered. She had received the private investigator's report yesterday and had spent all night drafting a letter to Elliott "Sander" Jones. This morning, she'd dropped it in the mail. She'd set events in motion, and if hurt was on its way, no one could stop it.

Chapter Eighteen

Candace
Thirty-one years ago

Candace's swollen hands looked like someone had blown air into surgical gloves. She assumed her feet were the same; she hadn't seen them in awhile. She could only sleep on her side, intermittently, when the little boxer inside of her took a break.

She forced her eyes to close, attempting the respite of a nap. Sander lay beside her, exhausted from an early morning practice session. As he approached the West Coast Surfing Championship, his practices were longer and often involved harsher weather with changing current and swell conditions. He always started during the low winds of dawn and determined the rest of his schedule by the tide tables, varying between high and low tides. He was good with numbers, calculating the exact times and places for the best results. She worried about him at times, but he was committed. Sander Jones was a man who made commitments and stuck to them.

Sander had been committed to her since the first day they'd met. Candace had asked him why he'd been persistent. He'd replied, "Any girl who sits at a table at a bar alone for hours probably has a story to tell." He didn't ask her story, had never asked, but she'd told him eventually, in broken pieces, the way she'd experienced it. He'd taken her back to her motel that first night and showed up the next morning to take her to breakfast. Then he'd offered her his room. "I bought a big couch," he said, "so I'd have a good place for myself in case I met a girl from Indiana who needed a place to rest." She stayed in his bedroom, alone, for several weeks, until she'd invited him in.

She fell into the rhythm of Sander's gentle snores, until a kick—or a punch—inside her said, "No sleeping allowed." Her eyes opened, falling again on the phone on the nightstand. She imagined the phone ringing. She pictured herself picking it up, saying hello, and hearing a distant, yet intimate, voice on the other end of the line. She had multiple scenarios for the conversation. Some of them involved her being happy; others were an outlet for her anger.

Candace pulled herself up and sat on the edge of the bed. The phone was too silent, the room too small. She heaved herself off the bed and pulled back the curtains on their window. She peeked at the alley past Sander's wetsuits that hung over the clothesline on their patio. She sometimes expected the scene to have magically transformed into an ocean view. She loved the vastness of the ocean, its horizon filled with limitless possibilities.

The tiny interior of their one bedroom, one bath home, tucked neatly behind a larger house, reminded her that her current options were limited. Another kick from the child inside of her confirmed the point, but she refused to allow those limitations to define her. Sander had helped her get a waitress job at The Cantina, which she worked until she was no longer able to stay on her feet for hours at a time. The manager now gave her a few days a week in the office where she was learning the business of running a restaurant. She had resisted business classes in college, but seeing how it all came together day-to-day created a desire within her to chart a career path. Leaving home had allowed her to see the person she could become and there was no turning back.

Art and Virgie had visited once. Their original intent had been to bring her home. Once they'd met Sander, who had a calming effect, they relaxed and seemed to accept her new situation. On their last day there, Art went for the bigger payoff. "A ring would be nice," he'd said to Sander. Candace expected Sander to defend himself and say that he'd asked and she'd put him off. Instead, he'd gripped her hand and held on. "Candace and I have to decide what's right for our family." At that moment, if a Justice of the Peace had been standing there, she would have said, "I do." Since one didn't appear, she'd had to admit she wasn't ready. Candace had barely adjusted to the idea of herself as a mother. Adding "wife" to the list of titles would make it all too heavy to carry.

She had hoped for a boy. To nudge the baby in that direction, she and Sander referred to the baby as "Little Eddie" after Sander's favorite surfer, a name that stuck after the doctor had pronounced the boy a girl. Candace had wanted a boy because she thought they might actually get along. She'd hoped not to mirror the conflict she had with her own mother.

Virgie had wanted to fly in to be with her when the baby was born. Candace told her she and Sander had it covered and they couldn't predict when Little Eddie might make her appearance. Virgie had agreed to wait, but now Candace almost wished she'd been more insistent. Candace was twenty, old enough for the responsibility she was facing, yet she felt young, vulnerable and oddly alone considering the child occupying the greater portion of her body. She supposed she wasn't the first woman to want her mother to be there during childbirth, although their happy family moment would likely fade quickly as she and Virgie took opposite sides on every issue.

They'd already disagreed on a name for the baby. Virgie had offered suggestions that involved an assortment of dead family ancestors, "names with pride and heritage," like Clarissa, Madeline and Elizabeth. Candace decided on Sandra Jones, after the man who took her into her into his home and his life and loved her so easily.

"Her last name will be Jones?" Virgie questioned. "But you're not married."

"She needs her own identity, separate from me."

"You can't create identity. It either is or it isn't." Candace could have argued her point, but her mother was probably right.

The contrary creature inside of her also had an opinion on the topic, sending a shock of pain through her. Candace grabbed onto the windowsill and quickened her breath as her birthing coach had instructed. It seemed so much easier in class. She held on until the contraction passed. Releasing her grip, she forced her breath to return to normal, holding onto a minute of solitude. Those quiet minutes would be precious when they added one demanding voice to their family. Candace was afraid those demands might overwhelm her, or that she might lose herself in the process.

She also worried that she wouldn't be a good mother, despite Sander's encouragement. His enthusiasm for the imminent arrival did smooth out some of the ripples of her fears.

Candace reached out and touched the nose of the oversized giraffe he had purchased. The friendly creature made the room feel even smaller.

She glanced one last time at the phone that was never going to ring. Next to the nightstand was a suitcase, already packed. She lowered herself onto the bed and touched the shoulder of the man who would drive her to the hospital and hold her hand as a little girl entered the world.

The vibrations in his breath stopped and he opened his eyes, his gentle gaze saying he knew before she said the words.

"Sander, it's time."

Autumn

Chapter Nineteen

Amanda

Amanda had been waiting for the right time to talk to her dad—or maybe she'd just been postponing it. She didn't typically keep secrets, but now she had accumulated two. And she still had the present Sandy had given her for her dad. She would look at the square box wrapped in gold foil—the edges smoothed to perfect creases—with blue ribbon and large blue bow on top. She told Sandy that she felt weird giving it him. Sandy had encouraged her to wait until the time was right.

"How will I know the right time?" Amanda had asked.

Sandy had tilted her head in that way she did when she was thinking. "Look for signs that something is changing—for better or worse. A change could mean he's ready for something different or because what he's been doing is no longer working. That's the time he'll be open to receiving the gift."

Amanda wasn't sure she understood, but she had been watching him, so much so that her dad had started to twitch under her gaze. "Is everything all right?" he'd asked her.

"Sure. Is everything okay with you?" They were two worriers, except she didn't need her dad to worry about her. She wished she could say the same. Last night, when Lacey's mom had dropped her off after volleyball practice, Amanda had noticed a glass on the counter, the ice half melted with the smell of alcohol. He'd probably meant to clean it out but had forgotten. She saw it as the sign she needed.

This morning, when he'd said, "Pick you up at Lacey's at eight," Amanda knew he planned to continue the ritual he'd set up for Wednesday—the day of her mother's accident.

On that day, Amanda and her dad had stopped at Rico's to pick up lasagna—the Wednesday special. He got the call while they were there. Wednesday had become like a cross at the side of the road where someone had died. Her dad continued to cling to her mom, determined to keep her bound to the earth.

Amanda saw it differently. She'd had enough dreams about her to believe she'd found a new life. She was gone, but somehow still present. Amanda saw her as floating above, like an angel. She wished her dad could see the same. Amanda had no idea if the small package Sandy had given her could make a difference, but she had to try.

Amanda left the wrapped present on the kitchen table with a note that said, "Open me," so he'd be sure to see it when he came home from work. Then she'd gone to Lacey's as usual to do her homework. She was having a hard time concentrating. She kept glancing at her phone, and then at the door, thinking he might call or show up early. At exactly eight o'clock, her dad pulled up outside. Her hopes for changing his Wednesday nights had already vanished.

She slid into his truck, putting her backpack at her feet. "Did you see the present?"

"I saw it." He put his truck into drive. "What's the occasion?"

"Did you open it?"

"Not yet. Why did you give me a present?"

"I didn't. Sandy did. She thought it might cheer you up."

116

"Sandy?" He went in alert. "Sandy, who?"

"Sandy Jones. I met her on my birthday at Ginger's. You remember me talking about her."

"Yes, I remember, but I don't understand. When did you see her?"

"I visit her sometimes after school at the store. She helped me pick out a dress for the homecoming dance, and she put it on hold for me. I'm going to buy it with my own money. Wait until you see it—it's black lace over gold polka dots. Sandy says it's youthful elegance. Don't you love that? I'll be youthfully elegant."

Amanda hoped her lighthearted, babbling presentation might glaze over the fact that she'd been talking with Sandy about him, which now that she thought about it, he might not like.

He turned onto their street. "I think I'm missing something here. Why don't you start at the beginning?"

"I saw you with her at the Fourth of July picnic. You like her."

He pushed out a breath, the way he always did when Amanda was testing his patience. "Why would you think I like her?"

"You stood really close to her and you were smiling."

He gripped the steering wheel a little tighter. "I don't remember standing close to her. We were just in line…talking the way people do when you bump into someone you've seen before." He pressed his lips together.

"See." She pointed at his face. "You like her."

He exhaled again. "You're stalling. What happened after the Fourth of July?"

"I went to see her at work because I thought, I wondered, well, you looked happy when you were with her, and then you broke up with Gwen, and she broke up with her boyfriend, and it seemed like maybe you two should talk or something."

"Gwen and I didn't break up because of Sandy, or anyone else. And if Sandy broke up with her boyfriend, it had nothing to do with me." He pulled into their driveway and turned off the engine. "Why didn't you tell me you were talking to her?"

"I don't know. I wanted to help, but then I started visiting her at Ginger's. I guess I liked having her to myself."

"But now you're willing to share?"

She considered mentioning the glass of alcohol, but he might feel bad that she knew. "I think it's time for you to stop going to Mom's grave all the time. I don't think it's good for you."

He scratched his head. "Let's go inside."

When they were in the kitchen, he picked up the box. "What is it?"

Amanda shrugged. "I don't know. Sandy chose it. She didn't tell me what's inside."

He held it up and gently shook it before he peeled off the paper to reveal a box with the Althea's Christmas Shop gold stamp, just like the one on the Santa he still kept in his closet. He opened the box and pulled out a small statue—a snowman. He held it in his hand, crinkling his forehead as if confused. Then he ran his finger across the red and blue scarf and smiled. "His face is friendly."

To Amanda, the face looked like all of her dad's other snowmen. If the hundred he already had didn't cheer him up, she had no idea why this one would, but he seemed to like it. "You should call her and thank her. I have her number."

118

"Can't you thank her for me?" He continued to stare at the snowman.

"*Dad*, call her." She took it one-step further. "You could go on a date."

"A date? You have us dating? We don't really know one another."

"That's why you go on a date, to get to know each other, right? I'm going away to college and I don't want you to be alone."

"You're not going away to college for another three years, so I wouldn't start packing your bags yet. You are growing up, but I'm not ready to date again, and I don't want to bring another women into your life. I made that mistake with Gwen."

"I liked Gwen, but she wasn't the one for you, and like you always say, it's okay to make mistakes, as long as you do your best. And Sandy isn't a mistake. I can tell."

He smiled, just a little. "You can tell, huh? All those years as a matchmaker have paid off?" He was teasing her, but she wasn't going to let him put her off.

"Dad, she's really nice. Chip likes her too."

"Chip?"

Amanda blushed. "Chip Dugan. He's this boy."

"Ah, I figured there was a boy. I think there have been some secret phone calls."

"Not secret, exactly." She thought about it. "Okay, maybe secret. We're friends mainly, but we kind of like each other, too. Anyway, we're not talking about me. We're talking about you. Chip saw Sandy at Bobo's, so maybe, when you call to thank her, you can ask if she wants to meet you there. She likes hot chocolate."

"I'll *think* about it. That's all I can promise."

"*Dad*, just ask her to dinner or something. It's only a date. Chip asked me to Homecoming and he's a whole inch shorter than me."

"Thanks for the advice, but I think asking Sandy out is a little different than going to a high school dance. And when were you going to mention the Homecoming dance?"

"I just did." She grinned. "So you *do* like her."

He blew out another breath and she knew she'd won. "I'll *think* about it."

"Great. In the meantime, I know a perfect spot for the snowman." She held out her hand and he reluctantly released it. Amanda went into the living room and placed it on the mantel next to her mother's picture. "He can keep Mom company when we're not here. What do you think?"

She thought he'd laugh, or at least smile, but the worried look was back. "I don't know, Amanda. Your mom . . ." Amanda could see he was struggling. "She was special."

"Sandy's special, too. She's just different."

"I don't want different."

His words didn't sound angry, but she was sure that was how he felt. She understood. She'd felt that burning in her chest more than once, but it didn't change anything. He was just going to have to accept it. "I know, Dad, but we don't have that choice. Mom wouldn't want us to be alone. She'd want us to be happy."

He studied the snowman. "When did you become so grown up?"

"I'm not so grown up. That's next year," she teased.

"Thanks for the reminder." He stepped to the mantel, moved the snowman an inch to the left, and then back to its original position. "All right. If you think the snowman belongs there, then he probably does. You know what your mother would have liked."

She did know, and her mom would have liked Sandy.

Chapter Twenty

Bill

Bill tapped his fingers on the table. What was he doing? Sitting in a restaurant, waiting for a woman he barely knew. Amanda, the matchmaker, had been asking him daily if he'd called Sandy. Each time, he said he was still thinking. Today, she'd put her hands on his hips in that way that reminded him of Ellen and said, "Gee, Dad, doesn't your brain ever get tired?"

Yes, his brain was tired. Very tired. All of his thinking had worn him down, so he'd called Sandy and left a message—a stumbling, nearly incoherent message about getting a coffee at Bobo's.

No matter how much enthusiasm Amanda had for the idea, Bill still couldn't quite believe Sandy was interested in him. Yet here he sat, like a teenage boy, squirming in his seat, waiting for a sign that a girl liked him. He could have dropped by her store to say hello and thank you, or hung out at Althea's knowing they'd meet somewhere between the Santas and the snowmen. Both options seemed equally daunting. It was less painful to sit here and wait.

As much as he hated to admit it, he was intimidated by her age—thirty-one according to Amanda, who read like Wikipedia when it came to Sandy. At least their ages were currently in the same decade, but that would change in a couple of years. He'd be forty, and with the weight of the last two and a half years, he felt every minute of it.

He massaged the back of his neck, and then stood up, deciding on a quick escape before he made a complete fool of himself. Before he could run, Sandy walked in the door.

Their eyes met, and he immediately felt self-conscious. She was so pretty, her hair falling effortlessly in a braid over one shoulder. She wore a skirt with tights and a sweater, and her shoes were short boots, similar to ones he purchased for Amanda because she just *had* to have them. Now he could guess the origin of her fashion need. Sandy's gaze locked on him with an unexpected force. He was finding it hard to move, even though he needed to go toward her and invite her to sit down. His feet wouldn't cooperate.

She took the steps for him, her eyes never leaving his, until she stopped in front of him. "You're here."

"So are you. I wasn't sure . . . Anyway, thank you for meeting me. Would you like to join me?"

"I would love to join you." She smoothed her skirt and slid into the booth. He sat down opposite of her. His palms were sweating and his mouth was as uncooperative as his feet. Words had deserted him. Fortunately, the waitress made a timely appearance in her 50s uniform adding a surreal element to the scene. "Welcome to Bobo's," she said to Sandy. "May I bring you something?"

Bill answered. "Hot chocolate?"

Sandy smiled. "Yes, please."

"More coffee?" the waitress asked Bill.

"No, thank you. I'm floating as it is."

"Pie?" she asked. "It's good."

Bill couldn't think of anything more 1950s than pie. He raised an eyebrow at Sandy.

"Apple," she said.

"Two." Now, he wished he'd asked Sandy on a proper date, as his fifteen-year-old advisor had suggested. He folded his hands together on top of the table, bounced them a couple of times, and removed them. "Thank you for the snowman," he said. "I never thought I'd see that guy again."

The smallest of smiles formed on her full lips—the same lips that had beckoned him to kiss them at Althea's six months ago. The urge hadn't diminished, only now the barriers were gone, leaving them both open and vulnerable.

"You stopped going to Althea's." Behind her words was a question.

"I stopped working on my Christmas display."

She leaned forward. "Bill, it's October! You don't have much time."

"I guess I lost my motivation."

"I saw your house last year. I didn't know it was yours at the time, but I remember all the intricate details of your snow village. You brought such life to it. Of course, it could have used some color, other than the one small Santa on roof. He didn't even have reindeer."

He could see she was teasing him. "Never really did care for red."

"Bite your tongue," she laughed. "I'm sure I could find you a fellow in a blue coat, or maybe a nice plaid. You certainly can't say you don't like plaid."

He glanced down at his shirt, self-conscious again. Gwen had never liked his assortment of plaid shirts, but Sandy had that gentle teasing tone in her voice, which put him at ease. "I might consider a Santa in plaid. I could put him inside the igloo."

She pressed her hand against her heart. "Where no would see him? Well, that would just be rude. I mean a man who dressed in his best outfit should be seen. I don't think you have an appreciation for Christmas fashion. With snowmen, you get a scarf, a hat, maybe a sweater and they're done, but Santas never go out without wearing a *suit*."

He laughed. "I'll see if I can get my snowmen in for a fashion consultation." He sat back, enjoying the gleam in her eyes. He hadn't realized how much he missed sharing his hobby and the joy in it with someone who understood. "So how many?"

"How many what?"

"How many Santas do you have?"

She shrugged. "Twenty."

He returned a skeptical glance.

She pushed out a defeated breath. "Forty, maybe fifty, if I don't count the ornaments."

"Ornaments count."

"But they're so small!" she negotiated.

He shook his head.

"Only seventy-five," she said with an indignation that reminded him of Amanda.

"Amateur," he laughed. "Which one is your favorite?"

"They're all my favorites," she said without hesitation.

He nodded. "You've got potential." The waitress delivered their pie and they both took a bite. "I can see why you like it here. The pie is good."

"To be honest, this is only the second time I've had it. The first time..." She looked toward the window, beginning to lose her spark. A second later, she giggled. "Oh, Bill, it's raining. Soon, we'll have snow."

Bill noted the drops dotting the window and the excitement in Sandy's eyes. "You're a winter girl."

"I am. There's nothing better than being inside the house at night by the fire and seeing snow falling outside the window. They always call it a blanket of snow because of the way it covers the ground, but I think it covers us with warmth from the inside."

Bill understood Amanda's fascination with her. "I'm sorry it took me so long to call."

She tentatively reached out and touched his hand. "I'm just glad you're here now."

He caught her hand as she started to pull it away. "Would you like to go out with me?"

"I thought we *were* out," she laughed. "But yes. I would like to go out with you. Do you think Amanda will want to join us, maybe for dinner?"

He had been concerned that the devotion had been one-sided, Amanda's attempt to fill the void of her mother's absence. It appeared that the admiration society was mutual. "We can ask her."

"Should we ask Chip, too?" Her grin said she was teasing him again.

It was his turn to put his hand over his heart. "A double date? That would be the end of me."

"So it will be just the three of us."

The three of us. He liked the sound of it.

"But you have to promise me one thing," she said.

"I think I can promise one thing."

"That we never have to come here again. I don't think I can listen to another fifties record."

He laughed. "We'll go for another decade. I hear the eighties are making a comeback."

"Shoulder pads? Oh, please, no."

They finished their dessert, chatting like long time friends catching up. Reluctantly, he told her he needed to pick up Amanda. He paid the bill, ran to his truck, and grabbed an umbrella. As he walked Sandy to her car, he held the umbrella over both of their heads. For a moment, they listened to the rainfall around them, and then he leaned toward her and found her warm, welcoming lips, exactly as he imagined they would be. He wanted more, but he pulled back slightly, seeking acknowledgement that she felt the same.

She pulled him toward her.

He dropped the umbrella and wrapped his arms around her. The kiss that followed was neither soft, nor timid. As she responded with the same intensity, the raindrops increased their frequency, matching the passion between them, blanketing them with warmth from the inside.

Chapter Twenty-One

Sandy

Sandy folded the hunter green cashmere sweater and placed it on the coffee table next to the set of makeup brushes she'd bought for Amanda. She always shopped early for Christmas, knowing that long hours at Ginger's would not allow for the slow, concentrated thoughtfulness she put into choosing her presents. Now she just needed to find the perfect wrapping paper to complement each gift.

"You *do know* Christmas is two months away." Candace had planted herself on Sandy's couch—again. To emphasize her point, she gestured toward the ornament tree, currently terrorized by flying witches and black cats. Candace's most recent unannounced visit was starting to annoy her. Her timing was worse than usual. She was also being elusive about the reason for the visit, which put Sandy on the defense.

"I know. *Only* two months away. I'm so far behind already."

Candace picked up the sweater that Sandy had just folded into a perfect rectangle. "This is a *man's* sweater."

Sandy plucked it from her hands and placed it on the table, returning it to its former shape, squaring the edges. "Of course, it's a *man's* sweater. It's for a man."

"Oh gawd, don't tell me *he's* back."

128

"It's not for Trent. He wears a medium."

"There's someone new in your life?" She gaped at the sweater. "And he wears a *large*? In *cashmere*? *This* I have to hear."

Sandy considered the consequences of providing details. Candace would have opinions that she'd want to share. Sandy didn't want opinions, good or bad. She simply wanted to enjoy all the moments she had with Bill and Amanda. She wasn't ready to share them yet—the moments or the people. "Don't you have to go to work?" Candace was wearing jeans and a body hugging coral knit top, an outfit that would serve her well in the tip department. "You look pretty, by the way."

"Good try. Now spill it."

If she "spilled it," Candace wouldn't approve. Sandy was falling for a man recently out of another relationship, unable to let go of his wife, with a teenage daughter that Sandy adored. Candace could present a hundred ways Sandy was going to be hurt.

"He's a nice man. I've known him since last year, but we only recently connected. Now shoo! He's coming over and I want him all to myself."

"When do we get to meet this green-sweater-size-large man?"

"I thought I'd invite him for Thanksgiving dinner."

"Thanksgiving's over a month away. How can I be judgmental if I don't meet him?"

"Exactly."

"Do I at least get a name?"

"Bill." Simply saying his name made her smile.

"Bill? His name is *Bill*? Is he dull?"

"Not a bit. Now off with you." Sandy scurried to the dining room, opened the buffet and placed the presents inside. She hoped when she turned around her mother would be gone, but she had followed her in, leaning against the built-in bookshelf separating the living and dining rooms.

"Okay," Sandy said. "*You* spill it"

Candace folded her arms in a protective stance. "Did you contact Sander?"

Her shift from non-participant to interested party sparked Sandy's old childhood dream of her parents reuniting, one shared by children of broken families everywhere, until reality chased it away, as it always did. "That's my concern and not yours. You're not involved anymore."

"I'm always involved. I wondered if you'd heard anything."

"Why do you want to know? You told me to let it go."

"And you haven't. You're stubborn. I would say you're like me, but I'm going to let Virgie take the blame for that lovely attribute. You're going to keep pursuing it until you're hurt."

"I know you mean well, but this is *my* battle."

"It may be your battle, but it's been my war."

Candace had never discussed her feelings for Sander. When Sandy was a child, she'd pry for details about him, and Candace had been cooperative—to a point. She talked about watching him ride a wave all the way to the sands of the shore and hearing crowds cheer for him at competitions. She laughed when she described how he squirmed and fidgeted when he had to wear anything but shorts and flip-flops, like a little boy dressing for church. But she never talked about how he broke her heart. Still, Sandy couldn't stop pursuing answers about her father, even if it caused her mother pain. For reasons she still couldn't identify, finding him had become too important.

Sandy deflected the topic. "I like your hair. It's darker now."

"I had some lowlights put in."

"Does Kevin like it?'

"I don't need his approval." She attempted to make the comment light, but the tension pushed through. Sandy suspected an argument. The hair color could have been cause or the result. Either way, Sandy wasn't asking.

Candace took a step back. "I need to get to work, but if you talk to Sander . . ." She paused, letting out a breath, "give him my best."

Any other time, Sandy would have followed that odd statement with a series of questions about her softened attitude toward Sander, but she needed Candace to go so she could finish getting everything ready. "*If* I talk to him, I'll tell him."

"And Sandy, take it slowly with the nice man. It wasn't that long ago that you were sitting in your old room, lamenting the loss of someone else. Just be careful."

Sandy wished Candace could meet someone as nice as Bill, but she'd probably chew him up and spit him out. And she hadn't been *lamenting* the loss of Trent. She hated to admit that Trent wasn't all that *lament-able*.

Once her mother was out the door, Sandy took a last minute tour of her house. Since this was Bill's first time here, she wanted everything to be perfect. She'd spent extra time fixing up her bedroom, even purchasing a new duvet set, because they'd end up there. She knew because it wouldn't be the first time that a bedroom had called to them.

The first time he'd invited her over, Amanda was out with friends. Sandy had brought a present—a little snow globe with a Cape Cod style house dressed for Christmas. One minute, she'd been turning the globe over, watching the snow, and the next, the snow globe was on the shelf and they had their hands all over each other, leading to a quick retreat to his private space. He hadn't planned the event. Sandy knew because when they made it to his bedroom, he had to shove clothes onto the floor to make room for them. She almost protested the harsh treatment of clean shirts, but instead made a mental note to take care of them later.

The second time was more calculated. She'd asked if they could meet for lunch on her day off. He'd replied that he typically didn't take lunch, but, for her, he'd make an exception. He'd suggested a picnic at his house. She'd arrived with a sandwich for Bill and a salad for herself. She had barely placed them on the kitchen counter when he took her hand and relocated them to a different room in the house. This time, he had neatly made his bed and all clothes had found spots in the closet or drawers. They had no obstacles between them, until an hour later when Bill received a call that a customer needed him on a job site. "Just as well," Sandy said. "It would be too easy to stay here." She had never experienced an intimate relationship like the one she was beginning with Bill, both physically and emotionally, and she wanted to continue.

Tonight, Amanda was off for her homecoming dance and a sleepover with friends, which meant she and Bill could have a sleepover of their own. She giggled at the thought of it as she put the chicken in the oven to keep it warm. She set her best china on the table and finished setting the table with candles and flowers.

Bill showed up at her door a few minutes later with a bottle of chardonnay. He wore a dark-blue sweater over one of his plaid shirts, seeming more handsome every time she saw him. He stepped through the door and immediately grabbed her and kissed her, shutting the door with his foot.

She eased out of his grasp. "I'll chill the wine. I was hoping you'd start a fire."

He started to grab her again when the fireplace captured his attention. "A wood burning fireplace? I miss those. The new ones we're installing are all gas flames, powered by a switch on the wall. Kindling not required. People don't know what they're missing."

"Kindling is required here, and a switch on the wall sounds good to me. I bet they also don't have to sweep out the ashes or pay for the chimney to be cleaned."

His eyes darted around the room, starting with her cove ceilings, lingering on the wainscoting and becoming fixated on the built-in bookcases. "But you love this old house, don't you?"

"Most days." They had found another shared passion. The list now included Amanda, Christmas, apple pie, old houses, and each other.

He knelt and ran his hand across one of the wooden floor planks. "Red-oak floors are the most durable. These will last as long as the house is standing."

"Sixty years, so far. I had the downstairs floors refinished, but the ones upstairs need it too. I also have some creaky floorboards that need to be fixed."

"Maybe I can help. Creaky floorboards are my specialty."

She laughed. "There have been times when I wished I had a new home, especially when I'm trying to do laundry in my closet of a utility room. But don't go and volunteer to expand it for me because I know what they cost."

"Personally, I think you should never turn down a volunteer, especially one so willing. I can tell you, you'll get a return on whatever you invest in this house. It's impossible to put these types of architectural details into the new homes we're building.

No one could afford to buy them." He made his way to the mantel, touching the leaf carvings in the wood. "It's always been my dream to rehab old houses, but the money is too good in building new."

"It's never too late for dreams, Bill."

He locked his hazel eyes on her and she could read his affection. She nearly threw her arms around him, but there was chicken in the oven and a salad in the refrigerator, and she was determined they would get through dinner. He stepped toward her, seemingly to suggest the opposite.

"I'm putting the wine on ice," she said. "Hold that thought."

He continued his survey of the house, wandering through the dining room. He stopped to check the "Nice List" grasped by the Santa in his sleigh, which still held its year-round position on top of the buffet. "I don't see my name," he called to her. "I'm glad."

She pulled the chicken out of the oven and set it to the side, thinking Bill's desire to be on the "Naughty List" might put the bird in peril of being blackened chicken. When she reentered the living room, Bill was working on a fire. The flames took hold. He looked up at her and said, "Now, why don't you come closer?"

She pointed to the dining table. "Dinner. Focus." She smiled. "How did Amanda look tonight? You took pictures, didn't you?"

He stood up. "You're a smart girl, but you're only putting off the inevitable."

"I'm looking forward to it, but now, tell me about Amanda."

He puffed with pride. "Of course, she had her hair done, as you suggested, into some sort of twist. She looked about twenty-five years old. I was hoping for pigtails. She said you helped her pick out the dress, which, perhaps you didn't notice, was strapless." He shot a mock scolding glance.

"She had a little sweater. Didn't you love the gold dots on the dress?"

"It had dots?" he laughed.

"You brought pictures, right?"

"I did, but you could have been there. Amanda invited you."

"I know, but you needed that time with her. There won't be another first dance for Amanda or a first time for meeting Chip. What did you think?"

He made a show of looking pained. "When Mr. Chip Dugan arrived, I opened the door and leveled my best fatherly glare. The kid didn't even notice. Apparently, Chip—I can't believe my daughter is going out with a 'Chip'—gets along *splendidly* with adults. And yes, he did use the word 'splendidly.' He wore an oversized suit coat, some fedora type hat and checkered canvas loafers."

"They're Vans," Sandy said. "Very popular. He's quite stylish."

"Oh, great. You're on *his* side."

"So you liked him."

The pained look returned. "Yes. I *liked* him, but what I liked most was that he's too young to drive alone at night and his mother had to take them to the dance. If I can keep him fifteen, I think we'll get along just fine."

"I'm sure he won't mind staying fifteen, since he wants to get along with you *splendidly*."

He laughed, but his eyes said his mood was starting to shift. Luckily, for her waiting dinner, a photo on the mantel sidetracked him. He picked up the frame. "Who's this? Should I be worried?"

"It's my father, Sander Jones." In the photo, Sander held a trophy in one hand and rested the other on a red and yellow striped surfboard planted in the sand. "I know—Sander, Sandy. It's probably the only time my mother lacked originality. I only have this photo and one other and an old newspaper clipping." The other photo, which she kept upstairs in a drawer, showed Candace at twenty, very pregnant, standing next to Sander, his arm draped casually around her. As a child, she loved that photo because it showed them as a family. As an adult, she could see her mother more like herself and started to feel guilty that she had taken away her youth, as if she had somehow been responsible.

Bill held onto the frame. "Sander's a unique name."

"It's a nickname. The story is that his name originated from his habit of riding the waves all the way to the sands of the shore. I've always found it ironic that a man who demonstrated such follow-through dropped out of my life before I ever had a chance to know him. I hired a private detective who tracked him to San Diego. I sent him a letter, but I haven't heard back."

He set the photo on the mantel. "Maybe you should go see him. We could all go. Amanda and I usually plan a trip over spring break. Last year, we went skiing, but I bet she could be swayed toward the beaches of California."

"You'd do that? You'd go with me?"

He took a step toward her and pulled her into his arms. "You might need to persuade me," he whispered, and then found her lips. She would say that he was the one doing the persuading because, in another minute, she wouldn't care if they ever ate dinner.

Chapter Twenty-Two

Amanda

Amanda wasn't one to brag, but she had been right. Her dad and Sandy had been dating for a month and he was happy again, joking as he once did and working on the snow village. As he assembled each section and adjusted all the moving parts, he also seemed to come to life. Sandy was good for him, and for Amanda, too.

Her relationship with Sandy was different from the one with Gwen. Amanda and Gwen sometimes ignored each other, but Sandy wanted Amanda to feel involved. On her day off, Sandy would pick Amanda up from school for "girl time." Sometimes they'd get their nails done, go out for a snack, or go shopping. Sandy *loved* shopping, and she was good at it. Last week, she'd laid out a dozen scarves trying to decide on the perfect shade of blue for one of her employees. Who knew aqua could be completely right and turquoise completely wrong? They looked the same to Amanda. Sandy and her dad were alike in that way. He could sand a piece of wood for what seemed like an hour to get it within a millimeter of perfection. Amanda supposed she should raise her standards, except she would be happy to slide through trigonometry with a B-.

Sandy hadn't spent the night yet, but it was coming. All the signs were there—the way he touched her arm and put his hand on her back when they were in the kitchen. He hadn't given Gwen nearly this much attention, and she'd spent the night. Amanda was waiting for "the talk" when he would try to explain how adults sometimes liked to spend more time together, but it didn't mean they were getting married or moving in together. Amanda knew all about it. Jennifer Grayson's mom and dad were divorced, and they both had overnight "guests."

Amanda was just glad her dad was happy, and she could stop worrying about him. Getting to spend time with Sandy was a bonus.

Today for "girl time" Sandy had picked her up outside the school with an apology. "My grandmother—I call her Virgie— called and said there was an emergency. I'm sorry, but I'll need to take you along."

"Is she all right? Should we call 911?"

"I *am* her 911," she laughed. "Her emergency usually means I've been neglecting her, which I suppose I have. I still haven't talked to her about you and your dad, not because I want to keep you a secret, but because I'm being selfish. Once Virgie meets you, she'll want to spend more time with you. I haven't been willing to share."

Amanda laughed. "I'm popular."

"Yes, you are. Now don't let her steal you away."

Sandy drove north of town, and they passed through the gated entrance into Morgan Heights, an old neighborhood with wide brick streets and huge homes that felt like mansions. "You're grandmother lives *here*?" Amanda had never known anyone who lived in Morgan Heights. "My dad loves this neighborhood. We come here at Christmas to see the light displays."

"Virgie's second husband, Art, was the grandson of Leo Morgan who once owned the only bank in town. His house was the first one built here. It's on the National Register of Historic Homes."

Sandy pulled into the circle driveway of one of the largest homes, painted yellow. "I *know* this one! Last year, the whole roof was covered in lighted snowflakes."

"Virgie carries on the family tradition of elaborate Christmas displays, except she pays someone to do it for her. Art insisted on doing it himself, except the roof during the last few years. I spent a lot of time here when I was growing up, when my mother had to work. We lived with Virgie and Art until I was six, when my mom bought her condo. I'm surprised she lasted as long as she did. She and Art were always at odds, but I adored him. I think my mother never got over being a rebellious teenager. It was natural for her. Still is."

"Your mom is a rebellious teenager? She sounds like fun."

"Oh, she is, particularly if she's not your mother. You'll meet her."

Amanda hopped out of the car and started toward the wraparound porch, until Sandy redirected her to a side door that led into the kitchen. Inside, the kitchen was a mixture of different eras, with new appliances, a green tile backsplash that could have been from some other decade, and a wall of cabinets painted white. In the center of the room was an island with a granite countertop. An older woman sat at a small table in an alcove sipping a cup of tea from a delicate China cup. She had striking white hair and eyes that matched her light-blue pantsuit and the blue silk scarf wrapped around her neck.

"You're looking well, Virgie," Sandy said, leaning down to give her a quick kiss on the cheek. "This is Amanda."

Sandy's grandmother smiled at Amanda, her lips covered with a pink lipstick that also decorated the rim of her teacup. "Oh, how nice. Welcome. Is this one of those Big Sister programs?"

"No. She's a friend," Sandy said. "What's the emergency?"

"There's a bug." Virgie pointed over her shoulder.

"A bug?"

"In the living room. A roach of some kind. He's quite large. I put a vase on top of him."

"Is he dead?" Sandy asked.

"He was alive this morning. I didn't want to take any chances. I thought if you took the vase off and he ran away, you could catch him and put him outside. I didn't want to squish him. Makes such a mess."

"Why didn't you call Candace? She'd make a better bug catcher."

"She doesn't call me back right away, but you always do. You're such a good girl."

Sandy narrowed her eyes, and said, "Hmm." She grabbed a glass from the cabinet, opened a drawer and pulled out a small piece of cardboard. She stepped through the arched doorway into the living room to survey the bug situation.

Virgie motioned to a chair. "Please, have a seat. Amanda, is it?"

"Yes, Ma'am. Amanda McAllister." She removed her coat and slung it over the back of a chair before sitting.

"Ma'am? Oh my. It's so rare to hear polite children these days." She tilted her head in the same way Sandy did when she was thinking. "Your last name is McAllister? What does your father do?"

"He builds houses."

"I see." She nodded slowly. "A fine profession. My Art was skillful with a saw. He replaced the moldings in the house. Pretty, aren't they?"

Amanda looked up. Crown molding covered every corner. "Yes, ma'am."

"Oh, do call me Virgie. Everyone else does. And yes. I know Art got carried away. There are moldings in every room, even the bathroom. Once he started a project, there was no stopping him. Now go see about the bug. It may take two of you. Did you bring a net?"

She laughed. "No. I guess I forgot."

Sandy walked back into the kitchen. "There's no bug, Virgie."

"Maybe he escaped," Virgie said.

"We had a freeze last week," Sandy replied. "Aren't all the bugs dead?"

"Perhaps this one was of hardier stock."

"I know you, Virgie. Candace told you I was seeing someone and you wanted to find out more."

She took a very elegant sip of tea. "Is it wrong for an old woman to want to know what is going on in her favorite granddaughter's life?"

"I'm your *only* granddaughter and you're not old." The bug picked that moment to make his appearance. He skittered across the kitchen floor, his destination under the refrigerator. Before he could make it, Sandy covered him with the glass.

"Bravo!" said Virgie.

Sandy scooted the cardboard underneath the glass and held him up. Amanda peered at the small beetle with spots of red on his back. He was cute, really, definitely not a giant cockroach.

"You called me to rescue you from this guy?" Sandy asked.

"He looked bigger this morning. Now you were telling me about the man you're seeing."

"I wasn't saying a word, but why don't you ask Amanda while I relocate this intimidating fellow to the garden." Sandy nodded at Amanda, cueing that it was acceptable to provide details.

When Sandy was out the door, Amanda said, "Sandy's dating my dad."

"I see," Virgie said again, following with another slow nod. "And what is your father's name?"

"Everyone calls him Mac, but Sandy calls him Bill. Even my mom called him Mac. He never liked the name Bill, but he doesn't seem to mind when Sandy says it."

"I see," she said one more time. Amanda waited for the nod. It came a few seconds later. "Candace mentioned that Sandy might be bringing a nice man to Thanksgiving dinner. I hope you'll also join us."

Sandy returned to the kitchen. She put the glass in the dishwasher, placed her coat on top of Amanda's on the back of the chair, and sat down. "I haven't invited them yet, Virgie, and they haven't said yes."

"My dad will probably say yes, but I go to my grandpa and grandma's. They're my mom's parents. Dad drops me off, but he doesn't stay for dinner. He says he wants them to have their time with me, but it's really because Dad and Grandpa don't get along."

"Why don't they get along?" Virgie asked.

"Virgie," Sandy said, "it's none of our business."

"Well, of course, it's our business. Isn't Amanda sitting right here telling us about it? It would be rude to not ask."

"It's okay, Sandy," Amanda replied. "I don't really know why, except Dad once said that nothing is ever good enough for my grandfather. I don't get it. My grandpa's nice to me."

"Yes, I'm sure he is." Virgie was nodding again and intensely studying Amanda.

Sandy noticed it, too. "Is there anything wrong, Virgie?"

Virgie didn't answer the question. "Oh, where are our manners? Sandy, take Amanda on a tour and I'll make more tea to go with the cookies."

"We're having cookies?" Amanda asked.

"Always," Virgie and Sandy said together, and then they laughed.

Sandy started the tour in the living room, with its high ceiling, framed by crown molding—of course—leaded glass windows across the front, a baby grand piano, and clocks. Everywhere. The molding had some competition for space. A grandfather clock announced three o'clock and all the cuckoo clocks chirped in unison. "Didn't all the chimes wake you up at night?"

"I liked hearing them. They sounded like home."

Amanda's home had been their old, two-story house in Lafayette. When they moved to St. Clair, her dad had wanted them to move into one of the new homes he was building. Her mom told him they didn't need new, but he said he wanted her to be surrounded by beauty. "I have you and Amanda," she'd replied. After her mom died, her dad had asked her if she still wanted the new house. Amanda thought it would feel big and empty. This house was big, but it didn't feel empty at all.

"I'll show you one of my favorite spots," Sandy said. She opened the door to the library. "I spent hours in here, reading in the window seat and falling asleep in Art's oversized chair.

Whenever I miss him too much, I come in here and he doesn't feel so far away."

"My mom had a lounge chair in the backyard. Whenever she sat in it, she said my dad had to bring her a drink with an umbrella in it." The memory did bring her mom a little bit closer. "Once for Fourth of July, he put a sparkler in her drink." Sandy looked away, and Amanda was afraid she'd upset her. "Is it okay I talk about my mom? It must be kind of weird for you."

"Please, talk about her anytime. I was feeling sad for your dad, and for you. For her, too, I suppose, as strange as it sounds." She inhaled deeply. "But we have a tour to finish."

Upstairs, Sandy showed her all the bedrooms, each one decorated with antiques and heavy curtains. At the back of the house, Sandy opened a door to a small room. "My bedroom." The room contained a twin bed, a chest of drawers, a table and a lamp. A miniature futon took up the last bit of floor space.

"There's no closet. Why not choose a bigger room? There seemed to be plenty."

"Because of this." She pushed back the curtains to reveal a view of the garden below. "In the spring, there are tulips and daffodils, and in the summer, marigolds, daisies and roses. In the fall, the mums will come out and at Christmas, the trees are wrapped in twinkling white lights. I've always felt like the garden was mine, as if Art, Virgie and the gardener did the work of seeding, planting, watering, and weeding, just so I could have this view."

"Wow," Amanda said. "A whole garden just for you."

Sandy laughed. "Art and Virgie never said it was for me. I just decided."

"You can do that? Just decide something is yours and you get it?"

"Not always. It doesn't work as well with people." Sandy lightly touched her arm. "I'm glad we're friends. Now, some cookies downstairs are definitely mine and yours. Let's go claim them."

Amanda had already claimed Sandy as hers. She hoped her dad would too.

Chapter Twenty-Three

Sandy

Sandy's arms ached from stocking a display of winter coats. She liked *buying* coats and *wearing* coats, but sometimes she didn't like *selling* coats. The corporate buyer had sent too many for the small space she had available, so every time she pulled out one, one or two more would come with it. On days like this one, she longed for summer with the breezy fabrics of shorts and tank tops that had no need to wrestle each other for space. But then it wouldn't be holiday season.

She'd rethink the display tomorrow.

When she arrived home, she was looking forward to a hot bath. She unzipped her boots and went through her mail, splaying it out across the kitchen counter, revealing a letter. She picked it up and read the address label.

Elliott and Marisol Jones
113 Carmel Valley Ct.
San Diego, CA 92108

Sandy's gripped the envelope, turning it over, then back again. She ran her finger over the return label, assuring herself it was real. She opened the kitchen drawer and slid the envelope inside. She couldn't risk an errant wind stealing the treasure before she could properly view its contents. Not that any of her windows were open. Her fear wasn't rational, she knew, but her mother had kept her father separated from her for all these years. The slightest interference might cause the tentative connection to dissolve into dust.

Sandy cast her boots and jacket aside and ran up the stairs, her feet heavy on the wooden stairs. In the guest room, she pulled the newspaper clipping out of the desk drawer. A group of surfers lined up, the participants in a contest thirty years ago. On the end was Sander Jones with a sparkling smile and wild blonde hair. She pulled the picture to her chest, knowing the contents of the letter could shatter any illusions of a relationship with a man who had once decided he didn't need a daughter in his life. Sandy's heart was racing. The dream could be gone in an instant. As Trent had said, they were strangers. The letter might only mean they would continue to be strangers. Nothing would change. She only wished she could convince herself it didn't matter.

She yanked off her dress and pulled on a pair of jeans and her favorite aqua sweater. Blue like the ocean, she thought. She slid into her black fluffy slippers, one of last year's Christmas presents from Trent. She'd bought him slippers, too, ones he'd kept in her closet to soften his step on her wood floors. She'd sent them with him when they'd said goodbye.

Why Trent was invading her thoughts now, she couldn't say. He'd been the negative voice, while Bill had been the positive, encouraging her not to give up the search. She thought of calling and opening the letter with Bill so she wouldn't have to face it alone, but this was *her* journey, and she needed to complete it.

She hurried back downstairs and turned up the heat. A north wind had blown through, taking with it the orange and yellow leaves of her oak tree.

She opened a bottle of Cabernet and poured herself a glass for the celebration or the comfort she needed to make it through the disappointment. She removed the letter from its safe haven and carried it to the living room, setting it on the table next to the ornament tree decorated with glass autumn leaves and an assortment of turkeys. After several sips of fortifying alcohol, she located her antique sterling silver letter opener—a Christmas gift from Virgie last year—and opened the letter.

Two pictures fell out. In one, an older version of Sander, his blonde hair darker and slightly receding, stood with his arm around his wife, Marisol. Next to them were their two children, whom Sandy's detective had listed as Gabe and Carmen, twenty-five and nineteen, their dark hair and eyes reflecting the Hispanic heritage of their mother. By some quirk of fate, Sandy's features were more like their mother's than her own. They all looked happy. A happy family.

The second picture was of Sander holding her as a baby. She recognized the pink dress she was wearing. Candace kept a picture of Sandy in a frame in the same dress. Sander looked comfortable with her in his arms. He'd kept the picture all these years.

She unfolded the letter—two pages on lined paper, handwritten, not typed, with words carefully printed.

The first words of the letter brought a round of tears.

My dearest baby girl,

Sandy closed the letter for a minute while she absorbed the meaning of the words. She reopened the pages, and continued reading.

Sorry it took me so long to write back. Marisol always tells me I think too much.

Sandy smiled at that one. She been accused more than once of thinking too much.

She told me to stop thinking and start writing. So I did. I have to say that I never thought I'd hear from you and I was happy that you sent a picture. I liked seeing my girl all grown up.
You were a year old when your mama left. I remember your first birthday and the way you had cake smeared all over your face. In your hair, too. Always loved that dark mop of hair you had. It broke my heart when you both left.

Sandy stopped. He was heartbroken? She breathed heavily, a swell of anger rising in her chest. Her mother had given a different account. Sandy wanted to stop right then and confront Candace, but Sander had more to say.

Now here's where it gets tough. I don't want to upset you, but Marisol tells me it's important you know the truth. How can I argue with a woman who has raised our two fine children and puts up with an old surf-dog like me? You said my name was on your birth certificate. I never saw the birth certificate, but I'm sure Candace had a good reason for doing what she did. Now before I say anything else, I just want to say that your mother is a fine girl, a woman now I suppose, and I loved her, and you, too. Those days with the two of you were happy and I don't regret one. But, honey, when I met your mother, she was already pregnant.

Sandy read the words again, and again. She felt numb. She scanned the rest of the letter. He talked about their days together and how she loved to sit on the beach and play in the sand. He'd added an invitation to visit, to meet Marisol and the kids and even offered a surfing lesson. She had to smile at that one.

As the numbness wore off, the feeling morphed into something beyond anger. All those years spent feeling abandoned by Sander Jones, but he had been there the whole time. She'd been sustained by a myth. The enormity of the lie threatened to undo her. Did Art and Virgie know? Did they fight for the truth and lose or were they willing participants in the charade? And why?

Almost before the questions found their way to her consciousness, she knew the answer. They were protecting her. There was another man—her real father—whom Sandy was never allowed to know. Again, she asked why, but that question would need to wait for an answer.

She calmed herself with a drink of wine—and another—and glanced around the living room that she loved. Her father had provided for her, allowing her to buy this house, but now she had to assume that man was not Sander Jones.

She wandered to Sander's picture on the mantel. He had a kind face. He'd wanted her, and that fact alone was enough for celebration.

She'd write him back. Maybe she'd go with Bill and Amanda for a visit next year. They'd have fun, and she'd be happy. She was someone's "dearest baby girl," and all the years of emptiness, wishing that Sander Jones had loved her, fell away.

Her mother, she'd deal with later.

Chapter Twenty-Four

Bill

Bill switched on the portable heater in his garage. He told himself he was there to put in some time on his outdoor Christmas display. He'd given in to Sandy's encouragement to "let the snowmen have their fun," but his mind wanted a different project. He unrolled a blueprint. He needed to take some measurements to complete it, but he didn't know how he could accomplish that goal without revealing his plan.

His plan. Had he taken it that far? He started to roll up the paper, reminding himself it was too soon for a plan. He needed to slow it down. *Relax*, he told himself. Let things happen naturally.

Before he tucked the print away, he grabbed a pencil and added in some more cabinets in the new laundry room off the kitchen. Sandy's stackable washer and dryer barely fit into the small space in her utility room with the hot water heater, so she definitely needed a separate room. He'd already outlined an addition for a master bedroom behind the dining room including an en suite bath with a Jacuzzi tub. He thought she would like a Jacuzzi tub after spending all day on her feet, but she might have to fight him for it.

He knew he was making assumptions and taking huge leaps. He couldn't seem to stop wanting those leaps, picturing him and Amanda moving into Sandy's house. They had already missed nearly a year when they could have been together. Time continued to nip at his heels, reminding him that every day counted.

As if tuning into his thoughts, his cell phone chimed and Sandy's name appeared on the screen. He smiled.

"I'm sorry to call so late," she said, "but I just got off work. We received a shipment of boots, and I had to put them on display for the weekend. Girls gotta have their boots."

"Yes. I know a couple of those girls, and when did nine become late?"

"Since I know you wake up at five-thirty, it is late for you. I'll need to apologize a second time because I was hoping I could stop by."

"You know you're welcome."

"Good, because I'm outside."

Bill rolled up the blueprint and put it in a container under the pegboard that now hung on the wall. He flipped off the heater and the light, and closed the door from the garage to his house. He hurried to open the front door.

Sandy had her arms wrapped around her black, ruffled coat, one she admitted sacrificed warmth for fashion. He pulled her inside and shut the door, folding her into his arms. "I'm buying you a parka," he said.

"It will look nice in the closet." She closed her eyes, and he heard a sigh of contentment escape from her lips. He stroked her hair, remembering the time when he'd forced himself to walk away. Now she was with him, exactly where he planned to keep her. He kissed her so she would know she was very welcome. She placed a hand on his cheek. "I'm feeling warmer already. Is Amanda awake?"

"She crashed. She was up late last night studying for a test."

"I'll see her tomorrow after school." She returned the favor of a kiss. "I wanted to talk to you alone anyway."

"Hmm," he murmured. "Why don't we go into my room? That way, we won't disturb Amanda."

"Luring me into your room? Clever, but why don't we talk out here?"

Bill surveyed the couch with a stack of clothes he had meant to fold, or hang up, before the blueprint demanded his attention. He hastily relocated the clothes to a chair.

"Those will wrinkle, you know," she said.

"Thank you, Amanda," he joked. "I prefer them wrinkled. Keeps me humble."

Sandy removed her coat, revealing a wraparound dress that hugged her in all the right places. She looked sexy as hell. She swung her coat on the back of the chair and unzipped her boots.

"My feet are one of the hazards of my job."

Bill thought of her in the Jacuzzi tub. He liked the image.

They sat on the couch together. He reached down and slid off her boots. He rubbed her calves, his intention to put off talking until daylight hours.

"Nice try. Very nice try, but talk we will." She waited for him to remove his hands and hold them up in resignation. She opened her purse and took out a photo. "I heard from Sander. This is his family."

He studied the picture of what appeared to be a happy family. "Sandy, that's great news."

"Yes, it is, except, according to Sander, he's not my father. He says my mother put his name on my birth certificate without his knowledge, and he's not really my father."

He redirected his focus from the idyllic picture to Sandy, whose face showed the disappointment of the revelation. "I don't understand. Why would she falsify your birth certificate?"

"Like most things involving my mother, I haven't a clue. I've considered numerous scenarios, including a one-night stand where she didn't get the man's name or number, except that she might have told me if that were the situation. My guess is that he was married."

"Did she say he was married?"

"She didn't *say* anything. She's kept the secret all these years. She isn't likely to break now."

Bill couldn't understand how her mother could lie to her about something so important or how a father could abandon his child. Sandy was maintaining her composure, but he was angry. "I think now is the time for her to break, don't you? How could she keep his identity from you? Are you going to try and find him?"

"That's my question for you." She searched his eyes for answers. "Do you think I should?"

Comments swirled in his head, ones he had the good sense to keep to himself. Most of them involved a deadbeat dad who didn't deserve to know her. All of them were accompanied by swear words. "I don't know, Sandy. What do you hope to find?"

"All these years, I've looked at that picture of Sander, the one I keep on my mantel, thinking he was my father. His face seemed so kind; I could never understand how he could leave us. Now I know he didn't, and I feel more complete because of it, but there's another part of me that's still empty. I have no idea who I am."

"Finding out the identity of your biological father won't change who you are, but it seems you've made up your mind. How do you plan to find him? Would your grandmother know?"

A small crease appeared between her eyes. "Probably. Virgie knows everything. I'm trying not to focus on how betrayed I feel. My mother and I—" she threw her hand into the air—"we have our own relationship, but Virgie..." She bit her lip, another mannerism he had come to know. "Virgie and I have always been close."

"Your mother didn't mention anything? Maybe she said a name, or dropped a hint of some kind. What about a photo album? People like keepsakes."

"Well," she said, shrugging, "she has me." She stared at the picture in her hand. "A photo . . ."

"Do you remember something?"

"I remember a picture. Maybe it's something. Maybe nothing." She offered a half-smile. "Let's not talk about it anymore tonight." She tucked the photo back into her purse and put her arms around him. "Now, let me give you my undivided attention for a few minutes before I go."

"Go? You just got here."

"You need your sleep."

"I'm feeling energized." He tugged at the strings that were holding her wrap dress together. "I think you should stay. Remember it's late," he teased.

"Amanda's here."

"Don't you think she should get used to us being together?" He kissed her neck and felt her yielding to his touch.

She took in a breath. "Bill, I know it's too soon, and I don't expect you to say anything, but I need to tell you. I love you."

He wanted to respond, but the words stuck in his throat. He felt like he was falling, faster and faster, out of control, and he didn't want it to stop. "Come here," he said, pulling her toward him.

Sandy placed her head on his shoulder, molding into him. He stroked her hair, until her eyes fluttered shut. He held her in his arms, his head buried in her hair that carried the scent of flowers.

He dozed off, and soon he was walking in a field of daisies. He saw his own hand intertwined with another, new and yet familiar. He looked up, surprised that the eyes that met him were blue and not brown. "Hey, Mac," Ellen laughed, flipping her blonde hair and running ahead through the field, her white sundress flowing in the breeze. She disappeared into the flowers.

He chased after her, and then stirred awake, his arms still around the willowy curves next to him, reviving a memory. "Ellen," he whispered.

Sandy twitched, and the movement jolted him. She pulled away an inch, the physical movement almost imperceptible, but the emotion of it creating a chasm between them.

He needed to say something, to repair the damage, but again, the words wouldn't come.

Chapter Twenty-Five

Amanda

Amanda tried reading the concentration that had settled into Sandy's face ever since they'd arrived in Lafayette. Last week, when they'd planned the trip, power shopping had been the goal. The list had included Amanda's favorite malls and Sandy had added a few of her favorite boutiques.

They had yet to step foot in any place resembling a shopping opportunity. Amanda didn't really care if they made it a mall or did any shopping, but the day had started out weird and had stayed that way.

When Sandy had picked her up in the morning, she'd been quiet. Her dad had been overly exuberant, promising to reward them with Peking duck at the Flower Drum Garden when they returned. He was trying too hard, the way he had been after her mother's death, attempting to appear as if their lives could be normal when nothing was normal. They seemed to be stumbling over each other, and Amanda hoped it wasn't a sign that a collapse was on the way. She assumed Sandy would perk up when they stepped into the stores already glittering with Christmas cheer.

When they arrived in Lafayette, Sandy asked Amanda if she would mind if they took a side trip to look for a park where Sandy's mom had taken her when she was a child. Sounded simple enough, except Sandy wasn't sure of the exact location. They'd driven concentric circles around the community college where Sandy's mom had gone to school. They'd pull over when they would see a park and she would scan it to see if it met the requirements. She dismissed each one, becoming more disappointed with each failed candidate.

"Why not ask your mom where the park is?" Amanda asked.

"The easy answer is that she's out of town."

"What's the hard answer?"

"I'm not ready to talk to her about it yet."

They kept driving and landed in City Park. A little arched bridge caught Sandy's eye. "It's probably not the right playground, but would you mind if we spent a few minutes here?"

"Do we have to go down the slide?"

"Slides, merry-go-rounds, and swings are optional. I just need a few minutes."

They buttoned their coats against the wind and felt the crackle of fallen leaves under their feet as they walked to the park. Sandy sat delicately on the edge of a bench. Amanda dropped down beside her, focusing on a little boy clinging to the jungle gym, screeching that he didn't want to go home. The mother made once last attempt at negotiating with her son before she performed the classic mother bluff—walking away. She assumed her own mother had used that one on her. The boy responded by running after her, rewarded with a bag of gummy dinosaurs.

"That was me when I was young." Sandy rubbed her nose with her mitten. "I loved to go to the park. I used to run over a bridge like that one, back and forth, and then I'd climb to the top of the slide and call out to my mother to watch me. Some memories are so clear, and others . . ." She paused, shaking her head. "When I was on the swings, I felt free, almost like I could fly."

Sandy had been buried in her thoughts, and Amanda wasn't sure how to respond, so she watched the leaves falling from a pin oak tree that was almost bare. The small leaves resembled falling snow, which made the wind feel colder. She wrapped her arms tighter around her coat. "My old house is near here," Amanda said to fill the silence.

"Is it? Did you want to go by?"

"Not really. My friend, Monica, used to live next door, but she moved away. The last time I saw the house, it looked smaller than I remember." She and her mom and dad had made all the memories they were ever going to make there. Sometimes pictures would pop into her head—her dad putting together a swing set in the back yard, her mom splashing with her in the plastic wading pool, the three of them raking leaves into a big pile and jumping into them. They were all good memories, but that house didn't feel like home anymore. St. Clair was home now. Her dad was there, her friends were there, and now Sandy. Lafayette had become a place to visit.

"You've been so patient," Sandy said. "Is there anything else you'd like to do before we shop? Your grandparents live here. Would you like to see them today?"

"They don't live in this part of town. They live in West Lafayette, near their country club and golf course." She didn't add that her grandparents would never live in this part of town, but it was true.

"Art liked to play golf. I suppose if St. Clair had a country club, he might have been a member, as long as he could take all

160

his Elks Club buddies along with him. They'd certainly shake things up." She smiled. "That's probably not a good thing at a country club. I'm sure your grandparents' house is nice."

Amanda shrugged. "It's big, but I like Virgie's house better. It's friendlier."

"Yes, Virgie's house is friendly. I don't mind driving to their house if you'd like to see them while we're here. I don't know if your dad has told them about me, but I could wait in the car or find something else to do for a little while."

Amanda tried to picture the scene. Her grandmother would open the door dressed in a nice skirt and blouse with gold earrings. Her first reaction would be surprise, followed by a smile that might be real or forced, depending upon her other plans. If her grandfather were home, which she doubted since he seemed to prefer being at his office or at the club, he'd be happy to see her.

"Grandma Lily doesn't like surprises."

"I might fall into that category."

"Sometimes I don't know how she'll react." Even in the cold wind, Amanda could feel the flush in her face. "Our move to St. Clair was a surprise she didn't like at all. She wouldn't come to our new house, not even for Christmas. Mom said she needed to get over it. But she didn't. And then it was too late."

Sandy lightly touched Amanda's arm. "Your Grandma Lily may have some regrets—we don't know—but I'm sure not having you close has been difficult for her."

"But we only moved two hours away. When Mom was alive, we came here like almost every weekend. I still don't know why she was so upset. Dad got a good job. We *had* to move."

"Grandmothers—and mothers—can be funny creatures." She shared a glance with Amanda. "You know what? This is our day out, so we won't let anyone spoil it." She chuckled. "I guess it isn't much of a day out if we sit in a park watching other people play. We should go."

"You never told me why we came here."

"I suppose I didn't." She slowly let out a breath. "I found a photo of me in a park like this one. I was about three years old. The picture had a little bridge in the background, like that one. I was sitting on my mother's lap and there was a man sitting beside her. I thought if I found the park, I might remember some details. I was too young when that photo was taken to remember, but I went to that park when I was older, too—maybe four or five."

"Does being here help? Do you remember anything else?"

She paused, sweeping the park for more answers. Her eyes opened wide. "I remember presents! I can't believe I didn't think of it sooner. The man in the picture brought me presents! Coloring books, a Lite Brite, a baby doll . . ." She gasped. "A red velvet dress with a matching puppet—a reindeer, I think. I loved that dress. I wanted to wear it every day."

"Who was he?"

Sandy closed her eyes and smiled. "Santa Claus."

"Santa Claus? *The* Santa Claus?"

She shook her head. "No. *My* Santa Claus. My very own."

"Like your very own garden at Virgie's house." Amanda was now as curious as Sandy. "What happened to him?"

She opened her eyes. "I don't know. We stopped going to that park and I didn't see him anymore."

"Wouldn't your mom know?"

162

"She would, but remember, I'm not ready to talk to her about it yet. So, for today, he's Santa Claus. Now, we should get our shopping done so we can get back home to your dad's Peking duck." She cringed. "That's not the one they serve with the head on, is it?

"I think they only serve headless ducks."

"That sounds worse. Maybe we should convince him pizza is the way to go. Pepperoni is friendlier."

"Like Virgie's house!"

Sandy laughed again. "Yes, friendly houses, friendly dinners, and *now* friendly shopping. Only friendly things today." She stood up and started toward the car.

Amanda headed in the opposite direction. She sat in one of the swings and called to Sandy who turned and hesitated for only a moment before she followed her lead.

As she and Sandy started swinging, Amanda flashed on a memory. She'd had been in the backyard of their Lafayette home on her swing set, when her mom came out in and squeezed into the other swing. Her mom had laughed and said. "Hey, why should kids have all the fun?"

As Sandy swayed next to her, Amanda propelled herself higher. For a moment, all three of them were there, swinging beside each other, completely free, flying to the sky.

Chapter Twenty-Six

Sandy

Sandy clicked across marble floors in the lobby of the office building past the modern white chairs formed in the shape of perfect cubes. She stopped in front of the tenant index. Her eyes flowed across listings for attorneys, title companies and commercial real estate firms. Squinting to relieve the glare from the floor-to-ceiling windows, she landed on the name that had been the object of the search. "Andrew Waters, Attorney at Law."

She read the name again, this time trying to form it into a man she could understand. According to the profile on his website, he'd spent the early years of his career with a prestigious, well established firm, specializing in family law, more specifically divorce. She was certain there was irony in there somewhere. His impressive curriculum vitae also included publications and statewide speaking engagements. He opened his private practice only two years ago, and the speaking engagements stopped. He seemed to have retreated, but not far enough. She had found him.

After her trip to Lafayette with Amanda, Sandy had felt uplifted, ready for the next step. During this return visit to Lafayette, one she'd made alone, that surge of courage had trickled away. She crossed the floor to the elevator, stepped in and punched in the fifth floor. A man in a dark blue pinstripe suit joined her, sliding in just before the doors closed, ignoring her as he pressed the lit number several times. She wasn't accustomed to seeing men in suits, but this office was close enough to the Tippecanoe County Courthouse to be home to attorney types. She had a new appreciation for plaid shirts and jeans.

The door opened and the man exited, scurrying into an office. Sandy paused when she stepped out of the elevator to take in the view of downtown Lafayette, wishing she'd asked Bill to accompany her. They could be looking at Riehle Plaza together or strolling along the walk next to the Wabash River, her arm locked in his. They could have gone to dinner, maybe spent the night.

Perhaps she was giving her insecurities too much of a voice, but she was regretting the urgent need to tell Bill she loved him. When he'd mistakenly murmured Ellen's name, doubt had found an opening—doubt about his feelings for her, doubt that she could be anything more than a patch over the gaping hole in his heart. He was grieving; she knew it, and still she'd pushed him. She was afraid to look into Bill's eyes for fear they would reveal a truth she didn't want to see.

She pushed away the thoughts, returning to the view and today's mission. She'd always appreciated the beauty of the area, but from the place she stood now, it was spectacular. She could understand why Andrew would have chosen this office space.

Andrew. She'd been calling him Andrew. "Mr. Waters" was too formal, and "Andy" too familiar. "Dad" had never crossed her mind. Since she'd discovered him, Sandy had practiced calling him Andrew until the name felt comfortable on her lips. Not that there was anything comfortable about what she was about to do. Sandy lingered at the window, telling herself she had the power to turn around, even though she knew she wouldn't. She forced herself away from the window and down the hall.

Inside the office, the receptionist— Ms. Hedrick according to her nameplate—addressed her. "Good afternoon. May I help you?"

Sandy had considered making an appointment, which would have made this moment easier, but her fingers had refused to punch in the number. "I'd like to see Andrew Waters."

"Your name is?"

Sandy hesitated. *What was her name really?* She stalled for a moment, choosing to complete a makeover of the receptionist in her mind, changing her curly hair into a sleek bob, adding some highlights, and replacing the black suit with a coral, silk blouse and an A-line skirt. Satisfied with the transformation, she replied, "I'm Sandra Jones."

She checked her computer screen. "I'm sorry. I don't have you in the schedule."

"I know, but I'd like to see him."

"If you're offering a product or service, you can leave the information and I'll see that he gets it." She had reduced Sandy to an unwelcome salesperson.

"I'm not offering anything. I just need to see him."

"May I ask what it's regarding?" She maintained a professional tone, but Sandy saw the urge to buzz security flash in her eyes.

"I'd really rather tell him. If he's not here right now, I can wait."

"I can schedule you for an initial consult." She punched the keys on her keyboard as if they had irritated her, or perhaps they were merely the recipients of her irritation. "How does December eighteenth at one o'clock sound to you?"

"Like a long wait. Can't you just call him?"

As Ms. Hedrick was preparing to explain why this approach wouldn't work, the door to the executive office opened. The object of Sandy's inquiry stepped out, shuffling papers back into a folder and setting them on the counter.

Before making her decision to make this visit, Sandy had stared at the profile picture on his website long enough she thought it might actually speak, but she hadn't expected him to be so tall and to exude such a commanding presence. His hair retained a youthful thickness, with more gray than brown, and he was handsome. Her mother always liked handsome. She took a breath. "You're Andrew Waters."

He glanced at her, the steeliness in his grey eyes startling her. It was obvious from his photo his eyes weren't brown like hers, but their dissimilarity widened the rift between them. Virgie always said she was the image of Candace's father, small in stature with dark hair and dark eyes, his Portuguese heritage carrying on through her for another generation. Now she could see it was true; her genes had rejected Andrew Waters before he had a chance to reject her.

A minute passed. She had hoped for a light of recognition in his eyes. In his defense, she had come in disguise. She'd wrapped her hair into a tight bun on her head. With black pumps and a suit jacket over a wool blend dress, all she needed was a string of pearls to complete the stern look. It was armor, meant to shield her from his indifference, or worse, blatant rejection. "I'm Sandra Jones."

The rigid stare that had greeted her softened. "Do you go by Sandra now?"

He knew her. That simple fact caused her to bite her lip, concerned she might have some sort of breakdown. She had told herself this meant Andrew Waters *had* to be her father, but she still wasn't certain. All she had was a photo of herself, Candace, and this man at some unidentified park. She uncovered the picture years ago as a teenager and had almost forgotten about it until Bill triggered the memory.

Virgie had tucked the photo behind another in one of Sandy's childhood picture albums and written his name and an address of a law firm in Lafayette, likely leaving her a clue. When Sandy had first found the picture, she'd considered asking Virgie or Candace about the man's identity, but decided to take the photo and keep it instead. Now she was here, facing the man in the picture. "I go by Sandy."

"Well, then, Sandy, you'd better come in." He handed Ms. Hedrick the file. "Hold my calls."

"You have an appointment at three," she reminded him, directing a sideways glance at the unwanted salesperson he was giving an audience.

"They can wait." He opened the door to his executive office. She stepped inside and accepted the tapestry-upholstered visitor's chair he offered. He closed the door.

She had played out the reunion scene with her father numerous times, but until a few days ago, they had all involved sitting across from Sander in a little cantina with the surf pounding in the background. He'd be dressed in cargo shorts, a t-shirt and flip flops, and she would be wearing a yellow sundress with her beaded sandals, ones she had already purchased for the event. The scene playing out now was nothing like the one she had imagined.

Andrew took the seat beside her, foregoing the position of power of the high-back leather chair behind his cherry wood desk. Behind the desk, heavy lion-shaped bookends flanked a set of law books. On the wall was a law degree from Notre Dame and beside it, a plaque that named him as a member of Outstanding Alumni from Purdue University. File folders were stacked precisely on one corner of his desk, balanced on the other side by a silver pen and business card holder set. An ordered desk. An ordered life. Andrew also dressed the part, with a pale blue dress shirt, silver cufflinks and a red silk striped power tie with a strict knot. He assumed a casual position, leaning back with his legs out in front crossed at the ankles, but he wrung his hands together, revealing tension that equaled hers. "How are you?" he asked.

"Fine." She said automatically, until the purpose of her trip demanded a voice. "Actually, I've been better. I just found out that the man I believed was my father isn't my father and he didn't know his name was on my birth certificate. It's possible that my real father has been living two hours away from me for my whole life." She stopped herself when she heard the bite in her voice. If there was going to be anger, she needed to direct it toward Candace. "Of course, I could be wrong. All I have to go on is this." She removed the photo from her purse and handed it to him.

He held the photo for a long minute. "Your mother didn't tell you?"

"Candace is quite proficient at not telling me anything."

"That's right. You call her Candace."

He did know her, or at least a detail she wouldn't have expected. "You still talk to her?"

He closed his eyes, and she wished she could see the pictures forming in his head. "I met Candace when she was attending the community college in Lafayette. She was working at a coffee house, one I stopped by every morning before I went into the office. She said she would have her own business someday. I always admired her energy and her ambition." He stared at the picture, and she could see the emotions playing across his face. "I remember this day. You had just turned three. You couldn't get enough of the playground. It was cold outside, but you didn't seem to feel it. You cried when we had to leave."

"Where was the park?"

"In Hillsboro."

She had driven through Hillsboro numerous times. It was halfway between Lafayette and St. Clair, but she had never considered that it was part of her past. The meeting place may have been out of convenience or a place where they could be invisible. Either way, they seemed to have made it easy on themselves.

Andrew touched a spot on the photo. "I bought you that coat and those boots for your birthday. I'd never shopped for children's clothing before. My wife. . ." He paused, shaking his head. "My wife does all the shopping."

He'd answered Sandy's question without her having to ask. He'd been married, which only explained part of the story. "If we were together then, where did you go?"

"We weren't together. I wanted . . ." He rubbed a spot between his eyes. She hadn't noticed before how weary he looked. "It doesn't matter what I wanted. All that matters is that I acted on the feelings I had for Candace, but I didn't go after her when she moved to California. When she returned, I didn't fight for you the way I should have. We tried for a while so I could see you, but you were getting to the point that you knew me. She said we couldn't live in two worlds, and what I was offering wasn't enough. In the end, Candace made the hard decision. She never wanted you to feel second to anyone."

"But I was second, wasn't I?" Bitterness snuck into her voice again. She was second in the same way Candace was second when her father had left her and Virgie for another family, which explained her mother's fierce protection of her.

"Don't confuse my weakness with your worth," he said. "I chose the life I built. I had the pretense of a perfect life and I had the career I wanted. I don't have any excuses, none that would change anything that's happened, none that would take away any pain that I've caused you. I can only say that we did what we thought was best. You had a stable home with people who loved you. You had a father, maybe only a picture and a name—his name—but it was more than I could give."

"You mean more than you were willing to give. My grandmother always told me not to judge, but I'm having a hard time right now understanding why you both kept this from me. Maybe it was difficult to explain to me when I was a child, but I've been an adult for a long time."

He nodded, seeming to give her words the thought they deserved. "Sometimes when you live a lie for so long, it almost becomes the truth. I know how selfish I've been. Every year, I'd think 'this is the year we tell Sandy. This is the year she looks at me and knows who I am.' And every year passed, and it never seemed the right time." He gazed out the window, but seemed to look beyond the view. "I am glad you came here. You're braver than I have ever been."

"I doubt that." Candace cared about this man, and she didn't give away affection, or respect, easily. He also seemed to be struggling, more than she would have expected. She decided to deliver the message that had started her on this quest. "Thank you for the money that you put into my trust account. I used it for the down payment on my house."

171

He waved off her gratitude.

"You helped me when I needed it, and I appreciate it." They sat in silence while she searched for words, but then she realized she didn't know how to fill the gap that had begun thirty-one years ago. "You have an appointment. I should go."

He looked at her with grey eyes that had seemed so hard before, but now held an unexpected sadness. "Please don't go yet. There's so much I want to say to you. I wish I knew where to begin." He turned his focus toward the bookshelf.

Sandy followed his gaze to two photos in silver frames. She blinked, trying to make sense of the images.

In one photo, Andrew has his arm around a girl whom Sandy instantly recognized. A beach provided the background with a lighthouse in the distance. Amanda had told her about a trip she'd taken with her grandparents the year before to Cape Cod.

The subject of the second photo was also familiar to Sandy. The same picture occupied a space on the mantel at Bill's home. It seemed impossible that Sandy's journey had brought her here, but the pictures told a story she couldn't escape.

"Ellen," Andrew said. "My daughter."

"Your daughter?" Her words were barely audible.

"When she moved to St. Clair, I thought having both of my daughters in the same city was a sign that we could have our chance. And then she had an accident, and . . ." His voice caught. He ran his fingers through his hair.

She was suddenly glad she'd dressed in her armor because she needed every tightly-woven thread, every hairpin to hold in the emotion that threatened to unravel her. The devastating implications for her future with Bill and Amanda were too overwhelming to process, but one single thought rose from inside her, and filled the room, until it was ready to explode. "I had a sister."

"I'm sorry, Sandy. I know this is all too much. Would you like to get some coffee? We can talk some more."

She exhaled, forcing her voice to a steady tone. "I can't." She stood up quickly.

Her movement startled him and he stood up with her, coming to life, like a slumbering bear waking from hibernation. "I'd like to see you again."

Sandy couldn't plan beyond this moment. Her feelings were blurring any rational thought. She'd come here without expectation, willing herself not to be disappointed at rejection. He was reaching out a hand to her, but it felt all wrong.

"I'll think about it." The truth was she didn't know if she'd see him again. She took a step toward the door, but couldn't leave until she had one more answer. "Why didn't you come to me…after the accident?"

All of the color seemed to drain from his face. "I didn't want you to think I was trying to substitute one daughter for another."

"A substitute," she repeated. Her fears about a relationship with Bill gathered like storm clouds. In a singular movement, she was out the door, dashing past Ms. Hedrick and her father's next appointment.

When she made it outside, she leaned against the cold exterior of the building, trying to catch her breath. A little boy and girl scrambled in front of her, chasing each other, wildly laughing, completely unaware that the world had just stopped spinning on its axis.

Chapter Twenty-Seven

Candace
Twenty-seven years ago

When she drove away from St. Clair that morning, the temperature on the bank sign read forty degrees. The sunshine didn't seem to be adding much warmth, and the steel bench underneath her wasn't helping. If Candace had been running around like her four year old, she might not feel it. They'd been here for nearly an hour. She was past the point of anger. Somewhere in the multiple times that she and Sandy had waited for him, Candace had slid into an irritated acceptance.

A little boy called to Sandy to follow him as he jumped off the slide. Candace wasn't worried. Her daughter wouldn't chance getting her coat dirty. She was particular about the outfits she wore and overly concerned with cleanliness. Sometimes Candace would encourage her to roll in the grass and jump in puddles. She'd once mixed up a bowl of dirt and water so they could make mud pies. Sandy had wrinkled her nose in disgust. Candace couldn't decide if Sandy took after the precise Virgie or the uptight Andrew. Either way, Candace was outnumbered.

"Sandy," she called. "Are you cold? Do you want your mittens?" Sandy stopped and stared at Candace as if she were a stranger. She shoved her hands in her pockets and turned back to her new friend. If Candace had stayed in California, Sandy would be playing on the beach while Sander rode in on a wave. They'd all go home to their little house, or maybe now they'd have a bigger one with a yard and a swing set. Sandy would have a father who loved her every day.

From the moment Candace told Sander about the baby, he had accepted and loved her child. When she'd told him she was leaving, he'd simply picked up Sandy, held her for a moment, closed his eyes and kissed her forehead. He'd put her in her stroller and took her for a walk. An hour later, Sandy had a new small stuffed giraffe tucked in next to her—a travel companion, she supposed—and Sander had the sad eyes of acceptance. "She's my baby girl," he said in a broken voice, "my namesake. I'd like her to know that she was loved...and wanted."

Candace had said, "I'll tell her," but she didn't know how she could keep that promise without revealing too much of the truth.

The truth came in the form of the hum of Andrew's Mercedes. His shiny black car pulled into the spot next to her Mazda. He stepped out in an overcoat. Beneath it, she could see a tie, which likely also meant a suit. He wouldn't be jumping into any puddles either.

Candace didn't rise to greet him. They no longer embraced as they once had whenever they saw each other. They'd stopped when Andrew started bringing Ellen with him to see Sandy. Lily had halted Ellen's visits, and the emotional distance between Andrew and Candace had grown.

Candace missed seeing Ellen. She was gentle with Sandy, pushing her on the swings, hugging her, holding her hand. Those were good visits, with laughter. Candace could see Sandy and Ellen growing up as sisters. She'd never exclude Ellen the way Lily had excluded Sandy.

Andrew sat next to her, his focus on Sandy.

Candace allowed him his moment before she spoke. "It's Saturday. Didn't you get the memo?"

"I had a client meeting."

He smelled good. She tried to ignore the effect he still had on her. "Must have been an important one."

"It was. The firm is going to be handling Tom Everett's divorce."

"The State senator?"

"Yes." Andrew rubbed his hands together the way he did when he was anxious. "Martin has asked me to take the lead."

Martin Broder was Andrew's father-in-law. If she had to make a list of the people she disliked, Martin would be at the top. He commanded a powerful law firm, and dangled the carrot of partnership above Andrew's head. To throw a prestigious client like Tom Everett at Andrew could only mean that Martin wanted to maintain control. Candace wanted Andrew to walk away from that job. Last year, he'd talked about it, and had made discreet inquiries to other firms, but the lure of a partnership at the firm was too strong. "I'm sure you'll do well."

He shook his head and took her hand. "It's not important now. I'm sorry I'm late."

"I guess Lily hasn't changed her mind about letting Ellen see Sandy."

"Not yet. She might let it go if I could say it was over between us."

"It is over between us."

"Not emotionally. Not for me. I can't tell that lie."

Candace could have said, "What's one more?" Except she understood. Staying with Sander would have been too big of a lie. Now he had met a woman who wanted a family and he'd moved on. Sandy would say, "Daddy's in California," in the same way another child might say, "Daddy's in heaven." The myth had been enough for Sandy as a preschooler, but as her understanding of the world expanded, so would her questions.

Candace gazed at Andrew's hand over hers. She'd always welcomed his touch. Since she'd returned from LA, they'd met in different places, and had now landed in a spot where they could pretend for a short time to simply be parents taking their child to the park.

Sandy squeezed into a swinging plastic horse meant for toddlers. She was small for her age, so she managed it. She was quickly outgrowing this place, while Candace and Andrew were stuck with nowhere to go. She thought of Sander and his faded t-shirt. *What would Eddie do?* Eddie would sacrifice his own life for a stranger. Shouldn't they be willing to do the same for their daughter?

Candace could feel herself pushing back the curtains she'd been too terrified to open. Behind those curtains were their lives as the "second" family. Andrew had yet to bring Sandy into his "real" life. Sandy would never look into the audience and see Andrew at her dance recital or see him sitting in the bleachers at her soccer game.

She also saw herself becoming smaller. The memory of the person she'd been before she met Andrew was fading into a collage of longing, stolen intimate moments, apologies, and nights alone. She feared her irritated acceptance would take root and grow into resentment that would strangle the love between them. That resentment would filter into Sandy who would find her own anger toward him.

Candace pulled her hand away and buried it in her coat pocket. "I can't do this anymore."

Andrew looked at his hand, seeming surprised to find it empty. "Do what? What do you mean?"

The singular expectation that their current relationship could continue uninterrupted provided the surge of power for the decision that had been silently waiting for a voice. "This! You. Me. This fantasy we've been living. It never passes the reality test. We've tried to find solutions. They don't exist. I made a choice to move back here so you could be a part of Sandy's life, but you're only Mommy's friend and Daddy is a picture in a frame."

"I'll talk to Lily again." He was too calm, lacking understanding that Candace was making a decision.

"It's not about Lily, or you, or me. It's about Sandy. I know what it's like to long for a father's love that never happens. The little bit you're able to give will only make her want more."

"Then I'll give her more. We'll tell her the truth." Andrew was making his own decision, different from Candace's.

"How does that look? What changes?"

"I'll see her more often."

"Where? Here? Where are you on Christmas morning?"

He rubbed his hands together again, this time with more vigor. "I don't have all the answers right now. Do we have to decide today?"

The idea that somehow, some way, the situation would work itself out had kept them from making the difficult choices. Their growing child was pushing them toward an answer. "If we tell Sandy, we have to tell Ellen and she won't understand why it's a secret and why she can't go to her sister's house or her sister can't come to hers. Once we tell the truth, we can't control who knows and how they feel."

"I can handle what people think."

178

"Can you? I don't think so. And remember, it's not about you, or me. Right now, Sandy is the daughter of a famous California surfer. She's the granddaughter of Art Morgan, a name that means something in St. Clair. She'll probably be strong enough to accept that you and I were never married and that you can only see her every other weekend. She might understand that Ellen is your first daughter and the most important to you —"

"Candace..." He tried to stop her, but the words continued to flow.

"It's true. You said you can't be a weekend dad to Ellen, but that's all you'll ever be to Sandy."

"You understand why I can't leave Ellen...or Lily."

"Sandy shouldn't be penalized because Lily's too insecure to allow *your child* to be part of your life. But we've already been down this path and we know it leads to nowhere."

"Sandy's my daughter. I'm not going to walk away."

The truth that neither one wanted to see stared back at them. "You already have. You just haven't acknowledged it yet."

He ran his fingers through his hair. "God, Candace, how did we get here?"

"You touched my hand when I delivered your coffee. There was no stopping what was going to happen. I have no regrets. I'm grateful for Sandy. She's going to be a challenge for me, but I can do this, with Virgie and Art's help."

"You act like this is done. It's not over."

"It is over. Sandy will never be part of your life, not in any way that matters. You'll never be able to introduce her to your friends at the country club as your daughter. Lily will never accept her. She won't love her. Martin Broder will always look at her as if she were less. My daughter is not less!" The tears she vowed not to release pushed through.

"Mommy?" Sandy held a weed in her hand. If there had been flowers, she would have picked a bouquet. Art's garden was her favorite place, and she couldn't be there without picking at least one flower.

"Hey, sweet girl," Andrew said, allowing Candace to wipe her eyes. "Come here."

Sandy climbed easily into his lap and put his arms around him, kissing him on the cheek. "Did you bring me presents?"

"Sandy!" Candace scolded. "That's not polite."

Sandy looked at her with her round, brown eyes and turned back to Andrew. "Did you bring me presents, please?"

He kissed her on the cheek. "I did bring you presents, please."

Candace noticed the large bag at Andrew's feet. He never arrived empty handed. She glanced at the soft leather of her favorite Frye riding boots that were last year's Christmas present. She'd allowed their relationship to continue on too long. "We'll open the presents later, Sandy. We need to go."

Andrew pulled Sandy closer. "Not yet, Candace."

"Not yet, Candace," Sandy mimicked. She wriggled free, jumped on the ground and ran away.

Andrew watched Sandy with tears in his eyes. "You know I love you," he said quietly.

Candace knew. She'd always known. The love had been enough to sustain her and bring her back. It was enough to take her away from a man who loved her and was willing to raise her child as his own. "I hate to say that your love is almost enough for me. Maybe I can find a way to live in the shadows, but Sandy can't. Look at where we are. We're sitting in a park in a town where no one knows us. This is tearing me apart. It will do the same thing to her. I can't allow it happen"

Sandy ran back to them and tugged on Andrew's hand. "Chase me, chase me." She giggled and ran toward the bridge, stopping to marvel at a robin that had landed on a rock.

Andrew fixed his intense gray-blue eyes on Candace. "I still want to see her. You won't keep her from me, will you?"

Candace couldn't break him completely, but the unspoken answer hung between them.

He stood up, straightened his stance, and went to chase their little girl across the bridge.

The Warmth of Snow

The Season of Giving

Chapter Twenty-Eight

Bill

Bill knew he'd find her here. Althea's was her refuge, as it was for him. As usual, she had sequestered herself in the Santa section where she was holding an ornament—a Santa face made to resemble a half-moon. She replaced it with that delicate touch he had come to know. She turned to a table and picked up a larger Santa figure, running her fingers over the fabric of the coat, smoothing the beard and adjusting the glasses. She sighed and set it back on the table, her shoulders slumping.

He slipped behind her. "You've been avoiding me."

She swiveled around, her first reaction a smile followed by something else he couldn't name. "Bill."

"That's me. What are you doing over here with all these dreary guys when there are so many happy snowmen just steps away?"

She glanced toward his favorite section. "They do seem to be having a party, don't they?"

"Always. Now, where have you been? I've missed you."

"I've been thinking."

He'd been thinking, too—thinking about how alone he felt without her. "Is this about what I said last week?"

"No," she said quickly. She bit her lip, one of the habits he'd missed seeing. "Maybe a little."

"Amanda said that you were quiet yesterday when you picked her up from school. She asked me if I'd said something stupid." He chuckled. "She knew immediately that it was my fault. She told me to say that I'm sorry." He reached for her hand. "I am sorry."

She waved away his apology, and his hand. "Calling me by your wife's name isn't a capital offense."

Maybe not, he thought, but her reaction said the opposite.

A few feet away, another holiday enthusiast triggered a dancing snowman singing an off-key animated version of Jingle Bells. Sandy gave the obnoxious rendition the attention it demanded, allowing her to avert eye contact. When the song mercifully ended, she met Bill's gaze for a singular moment, and then shifted back to the Santa, tinkling the bell at the end of his hat.

"Why don't we take a walk?" Bill suggested. "I'd like to have all of your attention." He placed his hand on her back and eased her out the door.

Outside, they both tightened their scarves and she pulled her mittens out of her pocket. She was the only adult he knew who wore mittens, one of many endearing characteristics. Sometimes he couldn't believe she had chosen him, although given her current reticence, he wondered if it were still true. He took hold of her mittened hand.

They walked in silence, their breath steaming ahead of them. Bill observed the lights strung from streetlamp to streetlamp as the city prepared for the annual tree lighting festival. Soon, a red and green wreath would adorn each lamp, and the oak trees in the median strip would twinkle with multi-colored lights.

He'd come to think of St. Clair as home. He could see himself having a new life here, if the woman wearing the mittens chose to see the same future. He thought they were moving forward, but she'd closed up. He needed to break through the barrier. "Talk to me, please. I'd like to fix this."

She shook her head. "You haven't done anything wrong. I've been thinking, though, that we've been moving fast, and we haven't allowed ourselves time to get to know one another."

"I'll tell you anything you want to know."

"I understand, but I've been wondering . . . I don't know, if it's possible that I'm only filling a gap."

Yes, Amanda, I said something stupid.

"From the minute I saw you," he said, "I felt a connection. If I had acted on my feelings sooner, we'd be having a different conversation. We understand each other, we fit, you love Amanda—all reasons we should be together." And if he could manage to say the three little words that insisted on being stubborn, he could add another more compelling reason.

Sandy seemed intent on avoiding eye contact with him. "When we met, you were still wearing your ring. I thought you were married. I questioned my own integrity because there were moments when I could look past the ring. Now I wonder if you're still that married man."

"It's a process, Sandy. Wearing my ring allowed me to feel like myself again, to feel normal, when I didn't know if I'd ever feel normal again. I hate to state the obvious, but I'm not married. Not anymore."

She looked up at him, and her gaze now pierced him. "I'm talking about what's in your heart, Bill."

He'd apparently done more damage than he realized, but he still thought she was overreacting. "We've only been together a short time, but I want us to continue. You told me how you felt, unless that's changed, and I thought we were going in the same direction."

They paused at the abstract statue that the city council had commissioned an artist to create, the multi-colored metal segments pieced together to resemble a rabbit. "I've never liked this thing." In his current frustration, he liked it even less.

"It's supposed to symbolize the new life of the city center, its revitalization."

Suddenly, the eyesore didn't seem so bad. "Yes, Sandy, a new life. We can have it, if we both want it."

"I'm afraid it's not that simple." Sandy sat down on one of the benches. "Tell me about Ellen. What was she like?"

He sat down next to her, trying to understand what she needed from him. He feared anything he said would drive her further away. Ellen had been kind, beautiful, funny, intelligent. He turned memories over in his mind, surprised that the details about Ellen were becoming muted, melding into one another like a collage.

He took Sandy's hand again. "She liked jokes. She could always remember the punch lines. I never can. She really didn't enjoy cooking, but she loved baking. Cakes—fancy cakes—were her specialty. She could have sold them, but she liked to make them for people as gifts."

She closed her eyes and bit her lip, perhaps forming a mental image. She nodded, appearing satisfied with her conclusion. "She was generous."

With those simple words, she'd captured Ellen's spirit. "Yes, she was generous."

She nodded again. "Do I remind you of her?"

He squirmed uncomfortably. His mistake had created a wedge between them and he had no idea how to fix it. "No. You don't remind of her, except in the way you treat Amanda. You're gentle with her, the way Ellen was."

She smiled, and he was happy to see it. "If I had to choose one characteristic to have in common, that would be the one I'd choose."

"Me, too," he said.

The wind blew her hair into her face and she attempted to brush it back with her mitten. He pushed it back for her, taking the opportunity to plant a kiss on her lips. She shied away and shot a look in the direction of her car. He was glad they'd walked far enough that she couldn't make a quick escape. She rubbed her mittens together and forced a breath. Bill braced himself for the words that might follow.

"I met my father," she said, "my real father."

She continued to surprise him. She hadn't mentioned a trip, so he assumed he wasn't far away. "He's here? He's local?"

"Local enough."

Bill thought that once she'd found her father, she would involve him. He assumed she would want his support, but perhaps it hadn't gone well, and she didn't want to show her disappointment. "What did you think?"

"I'm not sure."

Bill considered the timing. "I almost hate to ask, but since something seems to have changed, what does he have to do with us?"

She placed her hand on top of his. "I'm not ready to talk about it yet. I will say that I believe my mother loved my father, but he always belonged to someone else. If your feelings come from a place of wanting what you had—of filling the loss—it won't be enough to sustain us."

"Sandy, whatever happened between your mother and father has nothing to do with us. We're fine. We're happy together, or at least, we were."

She glanced at the sculpture of the rabbit, and tightened her lips. "I need a little more time. I need to talk to my mother. And my grandmother. I'd like to get all the family secrets out on the table so we can have a good look at them."

"I still don't understand how this relates to us, but if you need time to work things out with your family, that's fine. I'll be right here."

"Time apart, Bill. I need some time apart." She blinked back tears. "I can't think when I'm close to you."

He opened his mouth to make his case, but she put her hand over it. "And I need one more favor. I'd like you to have Thanksgiving dinner with your in-laws. Amanda said you don't get along with your father-in-law, but it seems like a good time to make peace."

She pulled her hand away and sat back, waiting for his answer.

He could feel his anger building. Bill was glad that Amanda was able to talk to Sandy about personal and family matters, except he wished she'd left this story out. Amanda always told him to "play nice" with her grandfather, but Bill said "nice" needed to go both ways.

"You want time away from me *and* you want me to make peace with Andrew Waters? He barely tolerated me when Ellen was alive, and since she died, I don't think he's said more than two dozen words to me."

"I know it won't be easy, but you're a good man and it isn't your nature to stay angry. Whatever happened between the two of you is in the past. He lost his daughter and nothing can ever fill that void. You share that loss with him, just as you share the love for Amanda." She leaned over and kissed him on the cheek. "Please," she whispered.

She'd made a decision, and for reasons unknown to him, they wouldn't be together on Thanksgiving. The anger seeped out of him, replaced by another familiar feeling. Helplessness. Except he wasn't helpless. He could change the outcome by telling her how he felt. He loved Sandy. He knew he did, but saying the words still felt like he was betraying Ellen. She would want him to move on, to love someone else, but he kept the words inside.

"How much time?" he asked.

Sandy sat back and appeared to do calculations in her head. "Two weeks." She paused, recalculating. "Three at the most."

He studied the strings of lights above his head that would come to life at the annual festival. He'd thought they'd be there together, wearing Santa hats like the two holiday enthusiasts they were. He'd also pictured her being with him when he lit up the snow village. He'd pass out hot chocolate while she greeted the families that wandered up to get a closer look. The next day, the three of them would go out to the tree farm and choose a tree together, stopping on the way back for lunch at one of the local restaurants. He could see them all laughing together. He'd planned every detail of the Christmas season, and they all involved Sandy.

"Two weeks," he said.

She stood up quickly. "I have something for you." She set off at a brisk pace.

He caught up with her and matched her steps. He stopped her at her car and pulled her toward him. She didn't resist, burrowing her head into his chest. He wrapped his arms around her, thinking if he held on long enough, she'd change her mind.

She pulled away, unlocked her car door and reached inside, handing him a rectangular box wrapped in red foiled Christmas paper and gold ribbon. "I want you to have it now." She kissed his cheek and ducked into her car.

As he watched her drive away, he thought of the blueprint of the remodel of Sandy's house waiting for him at home. It was a crazy dream, one that seemed to be slipping away. Still, he couldn't stop himself from mentally grabbing a pencil and adding a pantry to the kitchen.

Chapter Twenty-Nine

Amanda

They pulled up in front of Sandy's house and Amanda's dad left the engine running. He pretended to be watching the black Lab chasing a ball at the park across the street, but he kept glancing at the front door of Sandy's house. She wanted to grab the ball from the dog and throw it at her dad. Since the Lab didn't seem like he would willingly give up his prize, she'd have to find other ways of getting through to the stubborn man in the truck.

"Look, Dad, the General's already out." Amanda pointed to the four-foot version of Santa next to the brick pillar at the top of the stairs. "He's the first one Sandy ever bought. Did she tell you?"

"She told me." He kept his eyes on the dog. "What time would you like me to pick you up?"

Okay, things were just weird. Her dad said that he and Sandy weren't mad at each other, but they weren't talking either. They were "taking some time," whatever that meant. She thought she had them all fixed up, but they were going to need more of her attention.

"Sandy had to open the store early this morning for the Black Friday shoppers, so she said we'd make it an early night. Can you come back around eight?"

"Sure." His grip tightened on the steering wheel.

He was in bad shape. "I don't have to stay, Dad. We could get some dinner or something. Sandy and I are only decorating her tree. She invited me a couple of weeks ago, but that was before . . . you know."

He closed his eyes for a few seconds. "Yes, I know." He released the tension in his hands. "No, I think it's good for you to see Sandy."

She felt like a traitor, but she had to find out what was going on. She was hoping Sandy might give her some clues. "You could come inside, at least say 'hi' or something. Maybe you and Sandy could talk."

He looked away, staring intently at the Lab who had placed the ball near the owner's feet and nudged it forward with his nose.

Like the dog's owner, her dad needed encouragement. "Yesterday, you didn't want to stay for dinner, but then you did and it was . . ." Amanda searched for a word to describe their Thanksgiving, "interesting."

He blew out a disgusted breath. "The turkey tasted like cardboard."

"Are you kidding? It was the best turkey Grandma's ever made."

"She got it from a gourmet shop."

"Well, she made the green beans because I watched her."

"They tasted like cardboard, too."

He was pouting like a little kid. At any other time, she would have teased him. "So I guess you're not coming in."

"No, but . . ." He reached into the space behind the seat and pulled out a box. "Could you give this to Sandy for me?"

He'd wrapped the present himself. Not the best wrapping job she'd ever seen, but he'd done it instead of having it gift wrapped as he usually did. Sentimental, she thought. "It's the Santa, isn't it?"

He nodded and rubbed the stubble on his chin. For Thanksgiving, she told him he had to shave and wear a nice dress shirt. Today, she let him have his way, which meant no shaving and his favorite old plaid flannel.

"I'm sure she'd like it better if you gave it to her."

"I want her to have it now. I'm not sure when I'll see her again."

"You could see her right now! She's inside!"

He returned his attention to the park. The owner was putting his dog on his leash for the walk home. "I'll pick you up at eight."

She hugged the package to her chest. "Okay, Dad." Before she opened her door, she leaned over and gave him a kiss on the cheek, his stubbly cheek. He seemed to need it.

She trotted up the stairs to Sandy's porch, greeted the General, and rang the doorbell. Sandy opened the door and Amanda stepped into the cozy living room. A fire glowed and the white lights twinkled in her seven-foot tall artificial tree. Next to it, boxes of ornaments overflowed with red, green, silver and gold balls, tucked among a variety of bells, candy canes, icicles, and old St. Nicks. Santa figurines dotted the living and dining rooms, surrounded by garland and white lights. In the dining room, Sandy had already covered a second artificial tree in silver and gold ribbons and bows.

Amanda turned to tell Sandy how much she loved the rooms, but when she looked back, Sandy was standing in the doorway, slowly raising her hand. Amanda heard her dad's truck drive away. "You could talk to him you, you know."

Sandy attempted a smile, but couldn't quite make it. "Are you hungry?"

"Sure. Would you like this under the tree?"

"What is it?"

"It's for you. From Dad."

She held out her hand. "Thank him for me."

Amanda wanted to say, "Thank him yourself," but there was no way to say it without sounding rude. She handed her the gift and Sandy placed it on the coffee table, straightening the ribbon, reshaping the bow. Then she stared at it, as if she had x-ray eyes and could see through the wrapping. Amanda thought it would be easier if she opened it, but apparently, no one was doing things the easy way.

"Was it busy at Ginger's today?" Amanda asked.

Sandy pulled her eyes away from the present. "Oh, yes. We had a group at the door at five-thirty a.m. and we didn't open until six. We had our Ugg boots on sale, so we had a stampede when I opened the doors." She shook her head. "Merry Christmas, right? By the end of the day, I wished I was wearing a pair of those boots."

Amanda glanced at Sandy's feet. She had snuggled into a pair of black fluffy slippers.

"Oh yes," Sandy said, "that reminds me." She picked a present from under the tree. "You can open it now."

Amanda accepted the package, removed the wired gold ribbon that Sandy had tied into an intricate bow and tore the wrapping paper decorated with drawings of vintage shoes. Inside was a pair of slippers, exactly like Sandy's.

"We're twins," Amanda said. She plopped on the couch and set her boots to the side. She slipped into the cushy footwear and sunk into the overstuffed couch. With the fireplace, the halo

196

effect of the Christmas lights, the inviting sofa and now the comfy slippers, she didn't want to get up—ever.

Sandy must have heard her thoughts because she said, "Stay right there." A few minutes later, Sandy brought her a tray with a chicken Cesar salad and a Diet Sprite in a can. She'd added a cloth napkin and a glass filled with ice and a straw, the bendy kind. Amanda had confided in Sandy that she worried about her weight. She could see Sandy was trying to help her make better food choices. She appreciated it, but she could have gone for something less healthy like macaroni and cheese or a hamburger.

As if reading her mind, Sandy said, "Oh, I forgot the bread. I'll bring it. And save room for dessert. Chocolate lava cake. I picked it up from Karen's Bakery after work."

Amanda appreciated Sandy's sweet tooth.

Sandy returned with a tray for herself with the exact same portion, except she'd probably only eat half. She put a basket of bread on the coffee table and settled herself into the other end of the couch. "I need to get my third tree. I'll get a real one, a small one for that spot by the staircase."

"Three trees?"

"I know. It's too much, but I want the house to be full." She stared at the spot, almost willing the tree to appear. "I don't like empty spaces."

Amanda could see the same concern in Sandy's face as the day they went to Lafayette. "Did you ask your mom about the park?"

Sandy picked up her fork and jabbed at her salad. "No, but I found it. The park is in Hillsboro."

"Did you go there?"

"Yesterday. A funny way to spend Thanksgiving, I know, but it's what I wanted to do. I wasn't in the mood for turkey and dressing. Virgie had an invitation to a big dinner at her friends, so we let each other have our own holidays this year. We'll be together at Christmas."

"Dad wasn't in the mood for Thanksgiving either, but he trudged along." Amanda popped open the can and poured the Sprite into her glass. "The day was totally bizarre. First, Grandpa invited Dad to stay for dinner and Dad actually said yes. Once we were inside, Grandpa pulled him all over the house. He wanted Dad's opinion on everything." She put on her best Grandpa voice. "*Do you think I should replace the windows? Are these countertops outdated? Do you know someone who can remodel the downstairs bath? How much would it cost to refinish the floors?*" She laughed. "I don't think Dad works that hard when he's on the job."

Sandy took a dainty bite of her salad. "They're remodeling?"

Amanda shoved a chunk of chicken in her mouth. "Selling."

Sandy put down her fork. "They're selling their house. Why?"

Amanda chewed for a minute before she could speak. "They're getting divorced."

"Divorced?" Sandy eyes widened, as if Amanda had slapped her. "They're getting *divorced*? I'm so sorry."

She shrugged. "They don't seem to be sorry, even though they've been together like forever. Dad said he didn't how they stayed together for as long as they did. Sometimes it doesn't even seem like they like each other. Here's the weirdest part. After dinner, we all piled in the car—even Grandpa—and went to see Grandma's new condo. She says she's buying all new furniture and she's getting a dog; Grandpa's allergic. It was the craziest day. You should have been there."

198

Sandy offered a half-smile. "Having me there would definitely have added another layer of crazy. I'm glad your grandmother's getting a dog. That's good."

Amanda shrugged. "I guess so. She said Grandpa was getting what *he* wanted so she could have what *she* wanted. Then Grandpa said, 'They're not even close to the same,' and Grandma said, 'Not to you because you think you should have everything you want, no matter how it affects other people.' They weren't yelling or anything, but you could tell they were mad. I was uncomfortable, but Dad was almost laughing. I'm telling you, it was crazy."

Sandy picked up her fork and set it down again. "Maybe it's not so crazy. Your grandmother is right. She should have what she wants." She went quiet, staring at her salad and biting her lip.

Amanda thought adults spent too much time thinking. "What about you and Dad? Shouldn't you have what you want?"

Sandy opened her can of Sprite, poured it in her glass and took a sip. Amanda had finished hers. "I need a little time to think. It's not your dad's fault."

"What are you thinking about?"

"It's hard to explain, but don't worry. Everything will work out as it should."

Why were they making things so complicated? "Chip says it's better to be a teenager than an adult. I think he's right."

Sandy put her tray on the coffee table, as if one bite of salad and sip of Sprite were a complete meal. "You like Chip."

Amanda shrugged. "He's short. He wears crazy colored tennis shoes, these suit vests, and men's hats, the kind with the rim."

"He's cute, and he has a sense of humor."

"I like him," Amanda admitted.

"It's okay to like him. And don't worry about his height. He'll grow, and if he doesn't, he'll still be cute and funny and have a good heart."

Amanda didn't understand how Sandy could be so smart about other people's relationships, and not smart about her own. "Open your present."

Sandy scanned the box again with her x-ray vision. She moved closer to the box, knelt down, and slowly undid the ribbon and wrapping paper. Seeing the label on box inside, she smiled. She opened it, took out the Santa, touching the laces on the boots and smoothing his burlap jacket, even though it didn't need it. She placed it on the mantel and stepped back. "He's beautiful, don't you think?"

Amanda tilted her head, just like Sandy, and studied it. "I wouldn't call him beautiful, but he definitely has his own style. Not everyone can look good in burlap."

Sandy turned to Amanda, her eyes wide. "Oh, Amanda. You're funny." She blinked and her eyes filled with tears. "I've missed so many years with you."

The way Sandy fought to hold back her tears reminded Amanda of her mom. She found herself also feeling teary, so she stood up and gave Sandy a quick hug. "Okay," Amanda said, "enough of the mushy stuff. Let's decorate." She picked up a small box from the table that featured a glass ornament of a snow couple hugging each other.

A tear escaped from Sandy's eye. "It's new," she said.

Yep. Things were weird. Sandy and her dad might need a little time to think, but from what Amanda could see, they were spending all of their time thinking about each other.

Chapter Thirty

Sandy

Dessert was something Sandy *bought*, not something she made. How could she hope to parallel the crème puffs at Karen's Bakery, the tarts at Gourmet Delights, or even the apple pie at Bobo's? Still, she had to try. Maybe baking was hereditary and she'd been overlooking a hidden talent all these years. The thought lifted her spirits until she opened the oven door. The layers that were supposed to build the foundation for her cake were lopsided and slightly burned on one side. She pulled the pans out of the oven and set them on the stove.

She had decided to start with a simple layer cake, foregoing a mix, because she thought Ellen probably did everything from scratch. It wasn't that she wanted to compete or present herself as Ellen's equal. She wasn't trying to win Bill's affection. She knew she already had it, assuming he'd stick around through what must appear to be a slip of sanity. She just wanted to make a damn cake!

As she considered solutions to the lopsided layers that were supposed to stack evenly, the doorbell rang. She ignored it, hoping it was only a salesperson who would move on to the next house. The chime rang a second time, and a third, the level of impatience on the other side of the door identifying her guest.

Candace had spent Thanksgiving week in Florida, allowing Sandy more time to process recent events. While Sandy knew she couldn't put her off forever, she'd hoped for a few more days. Now she was down to stalling for minutes. She had to talk to her mother before she could tell Bill the truth, but she wouldn't have minded if Candace had extended her vacation a little longer.

Sandy opened a can of frosting—she hadn't been foolish enough to think she could make anything close to the perfection of Duncan Hines—and started spreading it on the first layer, thinking she could build up one side. The cake was too warm and the frosting melted and slid off. She sighed, and went to greet her guest who was now all but leaning on the bell. She opened the door.

"What were you doing in there?" Candace said. "Didn't you hear the doorbell?"

"I'm baking." Sandy turned and marched back into the kitchen.

Candace followed her, removed her coat and threw it across a barstool. "How did you get egg on the backsplash?"

Sandy peered at the dried egg, noting a heap of flour below it and the cup of sugar that was supposed to have gone into the cake. She sighed again.

"Why are you baking anyway?" Candace folded her arms. "You never bake."

"You're right. I don't." She picked up one layer of cake, put it on top of the other and dropped them both into the trashcan. She put the lid back on the frosting, thinking she'd be dipping a spoon into it later. "That's better. Now, how was your trip?"

"The first day was good, except for the sunburn. The second day was fantastic. Kevin and I discovered the virtues of Coco

Locos, which made the third morning rough, except it was still better than the afternoon, when I received a call from Andrew. I think it's time we talk, don't you?"

"If you're giving me a choice, I could put it off for a few more days, or a week, or forever, but I guess those options aren't available to me." Talking about it made it all too real, but reality was here, in the form of a failed cake and a mother who wanted to talk.

"No, they aren't. Let's go into the living room. I can't think with that egg staring at me." Candace opened up the fridge and took out two Diet Cokes.

Sandy started to reach for glasses.

"Oh, let's be daring and drink them out of the can."

Sandy opened the cabinet and grabbed two straws. "Fine, but we're using coasters."

In the living room, Sandy positioned herself at the end of the couch, sitting on the edge of the seat. She opened her drink, lowered her straw into it, and took a small drink. Candace settled into the chair, popped opened the can and took a swig, ignoring the straw Sandy had placed on the coffee table.

"So you and Andrew are still talking," Sandy said.

"We are *now*. I wish you had talked to me instead of going to Virgie. You couldn't have waited until I returned from my trip? It's been thirty-one years. Another week would have killed you? I'm kind of involved here."

"I did talk to you, and you told me to let it go. I couldn't let it go, and I didn't go to Virgie. She doesn't know Andrew and I met, unless you told her." Sandy had also been systematically avoiding Virgie, assuming she knew the story, which meant she knew Amanda's identity, and Bill's. When she'd begged off

Thanksgiving dinner, her grandmother didn't push for detail, but Sandy knew she couldn't hold her off for long.

"If Virgie didn't tell you, how did you know about him?"

Sandy reached for her purse on the table, pulled out the photo and handed it to Candace.

She took picture, taking a minute to examine it, and then lightly touched it with affection, similar to the way Andrew had handled the photo. She looked at Sandy, a question in her eyes.

"On the back."

She turned it over and read the words. "So Virgie did tell you."

"Not intentionally. I found the photo when I was a teenager. I suppose I should have asked about it then, but I put it away and didn't think about it until I received a letter from Sander. He told me he wasn't my father. He also told me he loved me. And you."

Candace put the picture on the table and kept her eyes fixed on it. "Sander was a good man. I cared for him, but not enough to forget my real life."

"So what was your real life?"

She sat back and folded her arms. "All right, I'll tell you. When I was nineteen, I was going to school and working in Lafayette and I met a young, handsome, charismatic attorney. He was separated from his wife at the time."

Sandy replayed her conversation with Andrew. He hadn't mentioned he was separated when he met Candace. He hadn't attempted to justify his actions or make excuses. That fact couldn't make up for years of denial, but it did fuel a desire to know him better. "I don't want a full accounting of your life," Sandy said, "but it would help if you would fill in some holes."

"Are you sure you want to hear this?"

"I need to hear it."

"I don't suppose you have anything stronger than soda?"

"I have wine, but you don't drink wine."

"I might make an exception." She picked up the can and took a swig. "Andrew and I fell in love. That part was simple, but he had a four-year-old daughter he adored."

"Ellen. I know," Sandy said with a bite. "My sister,"

"No. She wasn't your sister—not biologically. Ellen was adopted." She picked up the photo and studied it, allowing Sandy time to absorb a piece of the puzzle she wouldn't have expected. "Under other circumstances," Candace continued, "we could have been a family, and you would have grown up as sisters. Whether you were biological sisters wouldn't have mattered to Andrew or to me, but it did to Lily, Andrew's wife. You were the one thing she could never have. She adored Ellen, or course, but you reminded her of a dream she could never fulfill."

"So he went back to her?"

"He missed Ellen, but I also think he went home because it was his life and his future. When I went to California, he didn't know about you. I hadn't intended to stay, but then I met Sander and he made it possible. I did call Andrew later, and he asked me to come home. When I said 'no,' he said he'd come after me. I told him I was with someone else. I remembered too clearly the pain of my father leaving us for another family, and I thought I was being noble in not causing Ellen that same pain. But after you were born, there were many times that I wished I'd made a different decision or that Andrew hadn't listened to me and he'd come after me."

"That's why you moved back here," Sandy said.

"I wanted you to know each other, and I thought I could control my feelings for him, but neither one of us was good at it. It seemed impossible for him to leave his family then, which would have also meant leaving his business, since he worked for his father-in-law. We did try to find middle ground, but limited contact seemed worse than no contact."

Sandy thought of Andrew when he held onto her picture of them together. "Didn't he want to keep seeing me?" She would endure any pain, even seeing Bill if they couldn't be together, to be able to spend time with Amanda.

Candace dabbed at her eyes, and Sandy knew that Andrew had told the truth when he said it had been her decision. She removed her hand and squared her shoulders, hiding the vulnerability that had been visible only a moment earlier. "I couldn't watch you always hoping for more. I wanted you to have everything."

"No one gets everything, but I've had a good life. What about you? Have you had a good life?"

"I've had a great life. I didn't get the 'happily ever after,' but I had you and my work, friends, Virgie and Art."

"And Kevin," Sandy offered.

She shrugged, which was more revealing than any words. Candace's time with Kevin may have run out, and Sandy felt a little guilty that bringing Andrew back into their lives may have accelerated their ending.

"What about you and Andrew? What will you do now?"

"The same thing we've been doing for years—nothing. We thought we had a chance when Ellen moved to St. Clair. Andrew left his law firm. He and Lily separated. He wanted an opportunity with you. He was like the man I met years ago. Until..." Candace lowered her eyes. "Andrew said he told you about the accident. He was devastated. Lily asked him to come home, and he did. But he didn't go back to the family law firm. He was finally able to break away and start his own practice. I know I should have told you about him, but you had a father, or at least a picture of one in your mind, and until recently, you weren't talking about him anymore. You're angry and you should be, but trust me when I tell you that Andrew and I tried to find the best solution. We couldn't find one that made everyone happy, so we went for the one that we thought involved the least amount of hurt."

Sandy considered the irony of Candace not wanting her to be hurt, when all she could feel now was pain. "From the moment you and Andrew got together, there was nothing you could do to prevent hurt from happening. I was always going to be hurt in some way, and so were Lily and Ellen. So were you. I'm not judging either of you. I'm only saying that you can't stop truth and you can't stop it from hurting." If there had been a way to stop the truth, Sandy would be the first in line. "I don't understand, though, why he stayed with Lily all those years."

Candace stood up and took a step toward the mantel, eyeing the burlap-coated Santa. "Guilt. Habit. Fear." She picked up the Santa, flicking the shoelaces. "Love at the beginning, I suppose, but I think they forgot about it long ago. He has regrets. So do I. But our regrets won't change the situation. Ellen had a daughter, Amanda." Candace said, bringing another truth into the situation. "She's fifteen."

It was Sandy's turn to know something Candace didn't, but she'd find out soon enough that Sandy not only knew Amanda, but that she already loved her. "We'll need to tell Amanda's father," Sandy said, "and he'll have to decide if he wants to talk to her about it. But not yet. I need a little more time." She plucked the Santa from Candace's hand, repositioning him on the mantel. "You might have dropped it," she said.

"What's so special about it? You've got a thousand others."

Sandy calculated the number of Santas she'd added to her collection in the past couple of months, including Bill's addition. "Just over fifty, plus the ornaments."

"Okay. Fifty plus a thousand ornaments. Why is this one special?"

She gazed at the prized object. "It was a gift."

"A gift. Perhaps from the infamous Bill, whom we have yet to meet. Why are you hiding him?" She narrowed her eyes. "He's not married, is he?"

Sandy had been successfully restraining her anger, but Candace was pushing her limits. "He's not married, but he's not free either. I can't talk about it right now." Sandy had always thought she and Candace had very little in common. Now she wondered if she were seeing herself twenty years from now, still in love with a man who might never be hers. "I have somewhere I need to be, but before I go, I have one more question. Did Ellen know she was adopted?"

"Yes, she knew. Why?"

"And she never met her real parents?"

"I don't believe so."

"I think Ellen and I would have understood each other, and we would have been close. Like sisters."

"She was a sweet girl. I know Andrew and I made mistakes and we should have told you sooner, but honestly, I will never regret that you did not have to experience the pain that her death brought to her family."

"Maybe not then, but the pain of loss doesn't have an expiration date. And Ellen was my family. I have to go now." She opened the front door.

Candace took the cue and retrieved her coat. "Don't be too hard on Virgie. She wanted me to tell you about Andrew a long time ago, but I think she realized how you having a relationship with Andrew when I couldn't would hurt me. You're her granddaughter, but I'm her daughter. She was protecting both of us. She always said I couldn't keep Andrew a secret forever, and you deserved to know your father."

The words sounded exactly like Virgie. The initial anger she had toward her had already faded, and she was happy to know her grandmother had always been on the side of the truth.

Candace placed her hand on Sandy's hair and smoothed it, the way she did when Sandy was a child. "Don't let this eat you up, baby." She turned to the door and was gone.

Sandy took a few minutes to compose herself. She grabbed her own coat and hurried to her car, concerned she would be losing daylight soon. She'd made the decision to visit Ellen's grave days ago, but she'd been taking it in stages, driving by the cemetery several times, and stopping by the office yesterday to ask about the location of the grave. Now, it seemed she couldn't wait a moment longer.

She drove across town as quickly as the uncooperative streetlights would allow and parked at the nearest parking space. She stepped out of her car and kept her eyes on the stone angel in the middle of the grounds.

On the path toward her destination, she could see Art's grave on the other side of the angel. All those years, he'd kept the secret, too. She assumed he'd believed he was protecting her, too. She stepped closer to Ellen's grave and saw a pinwheel stuck in a vase of silk daisies. The flutter of a similar pinwheel had encouraged her to begin this journey. "Okay, Art," she said. "I hear you."

She approached Ellen's marker cautiously wishing she had picked up a bouquet of flowers as she had planned. They wouldn't have lasted the night, but she would have felt better knowing they were there. She hovered above the marker for a minute before lowering herself to her knees. She pulled off her mitten and ran her fingers across the cold stone etching of Ellen's name—*Ellen Waters McAllister*. She lightly touched the words below. *Wife. Mother. Daughter.*

She inhaled sharply, feeling the bite of the cold in her lungs. She hoped being here would bring her closer to the sister she could have had, but all she felt was a dark well of grief. Not so much for herself, but for Bill and Amanda. For Andrew. For Candace. She was sharing the grief of the people she loved. Her family.

She felt the tears on her cheeks, allowing them to flow freely until she had none left inside.

Chapter Thirty-One

Bill

Bill massaged his left hand, imagining his wedding ring on his finger again. Since Sandy had suggested he might be confusing his affection for her with the need to fill his loss, Ellen had been present in his mind. He would have dismissed the idea completely, if not for his minor slip in saying Ellen's name, and the doubt that now seemed to plague him.

Was he only reacting to Ellen's memory? Was it possible that Sandy was only filling an empty space? God, he hoped not. He hoped he was a better man, one who wouldn't take advantage of a woman's affection. With Gwen, he knew he needed to take it slowly, but with Sandy, maybe they'd fallen too fast.

The first time he invited her to his house, she'd brought a gift—a snow globe with a picture-perfect two-story Cape Cod style house, surrounded by trees. "I know you like old houses," she said, smiling and turning the globe upside down to watch the snowfall. When it all settled to the bottom, she'd turn it over again. "And it's always winter there, so you can have snow whenever you want." She glanced up and saw him staring at her. He felt her mood shift, as did his. He lost himself in her deep brown eyes that were asking a question for which he already had an answer. He pulled her toward him and the passion that had played between them exploded into a single kiss, leading to another, and soon, into his bedroom.

He pushed the memory of their passion aside, focusing instead on the image of Sandy mesmerized by the tiny house in the falling snow. After Amanda told him about her grandmother's house in Morgan Heights, he could understand her fascination with the globe—just his luck to fall for another society girl. He shook his head at the antiquated term, but it fit. Ellen hadn't come from "old" money like Sandy, but there had been enough of the new stuff to make Ellen's father think she deserved someone with better prospects than Bill.

God, he hated that he'd given Andrew Waters a chance to gloat. For the first years of their marriage, he and Ellen had financial difficulties with breaks in his employment when new construction was on hold. He filled in with remodeling jobs. One year he owed most of his winter income to storms that kept him repairing roofs and rebuilding fences. He winced at the memory of the times when Ellen was the only one putting money in the bank to cover their expenses.

When they moved to St. Clair, they were only going to live in their small ranch house for a year until his company completed the first phase of the planned development. He and Ellen had chosen their model—the largest of the floor plans—and were deciding on upgrades when their lives were irrevocably altered. Now he couldn't handle the thought of moving into one of the mass-produced homes he built, even though the income from them sustained their lifestyle. He had to acknowledge that he had never wanted the sparkle of new. The home had been for Ellen and Amanda, to allow them the joy of creating their home just as they wanted it to be. He had moved them away from their family and friends to St. Clair for his steady job and paycheck, and he wanted them to have something in return.

The other benefit to moving his family into the most prestigious model was that he could finally show Andrew that Ellen had made the right choice in marrying him. What a joke. The only positive he could see was that he no longer gave a damn about Andrew's opinion, or anyone else's, except Amanda's, and now Sandy's.

Sandy. Maybe she'd been too hasty in her declaration, and now realized he wasn't the one for her. The doubts kept him going in circles, and the circles had him visiting Ellen's grave more often. He couldn't decide if the visits made it better or worse. He felt he needed to do *something*, so he'd started there. Sandy said he was still in love with Ellen, but when he stood beside her grave, he just felt alone, as if he'd lost the love of his life for a second time.

He had forced himself to continue working on his Christmas display, thinking some signs of the holiday cheer would clear the fog in his head. When those efforts brought him no peace, he'd taken Amanda to the Christmas tree farm where they wandered around for an hour trying to find the perfect tree. Perfect was never going to happen. They finally settled on one that would fit on a tabletop, the larger versions proving too intimidating to tackle.

"Sandy has three trees, two artificial and one real one," Amanda told him as they drove away from the farm. "She says she must have a real one, but artificial trees hold the ornaments better. And they're prelit."

"Did you want an artificial tree?" he'd asked. "You could have told me. We could have bought one." *And prelit would have been easier.*

"I thought we were cutting our own tree because that's what we did when Mom was alive. It's tradition. I thought it's what you wanted."

"Amanda," he'd replied evenly, "I know I'm the dad and I'm supposed to know everything, but I can tell you that right now, I don't have a clue about what I want."

"Sandy says that it's okay to change traditions, as long as we hold onto the memories."

Bill wanted to scream that if Sandy had allowed them to make any memories, then he could have held onto them, but Amanda didn't need to hear it.

He needed to calm down. Even though a week had passed without hearing from her, they were going to talk. She was going to tell him why she had pulled away, and he was going to set all of his doubts aside. They were going to work it out, or so he continued to tell himself.

Tonight, he revived another tradition—a drink at The Rusty Nail. He had hoped that Candace wouldn't be working so he could have his beer in solitude, but he was destined for company. Candace had greeted him when he walked in, poured his drink and left him alone. Now she was calling to him from the other end of the bar.

"Hey, Mac, you want another beer?"

"No, thanks. I have to pick up my daughter. I need to go soon."

Candace poured a mixed drink and delivered it, making her way toward Bill. She leaned against the counter behind her and crossed her arms. "How's she doing, your daughter, I mean?"

Bill tried to recall if he'd discussed Amanda with her; nothing came to mind. "She's all right. She's a sophomore this year, so she has even more activities."

Candace took a step toward him, placing her hands of the bar. Bill focused on the color of her eyes. Deep brown. He'd never noticed before.

"If she's all right," she said, "then she's doing better than you."

Bill considered playing innocent, but he was a wreck, and he probably looked it. "It's been rough."

"Do you want to talk about it? I *am* a bartender."

Bill preferred his anonymity, but Candace had always given him special attention, ignoring his best efforts to sulk in private. "My wife was killed in a car accident a couple of years ago." He was leaving out the important details of recent events, but Ellen's death was the beginning. He didn't know the ending.

She took Bill's half-empty glass and dumped it. "Hate to see a man drink warm beer." She poured a new beer in a cold glass and set it in front of him. "I know about your wife. When you first started coming in here, I wanted to give you your privacy. I figured you'd open up about it when you were ready, but you never have." She stopped short of apologizing for not mentioning it sooner, but she spoke gently to him, as she always had.

He always thought she seemed concerned about him. Now he knew it was true. Bill was irritated. All this time, he thought he could mourn in peace, but she'd been there, silently watching him. This place had been a refuge for him, but now he felt exposed. "Did you read about the accident? How did you know she was my wife?"

She retreated slightly. "I'd like to talk about it when we're not here, but I'll just tell you that I know Andrew."

"Andrew?" Bill went into high alert. "Andrew Waters?"

"Yes," she said, almost in a whisper, "I really do need to talk with you."

Bill held up his hand. "You knew Andrew all this time and you didn't mention it?" He didn't attempt to hide his anger. "I really don't want to talk about my father-in-law, with you or anyone else. Sandy. . ." Just saying her name created a landslide of emotion. "Sandy wanted me to make peace with him, but I don't see that happening. My holiday spirit doesn't extend that far. I don't know what you have to say, but I'm not up for a conversation that involves Andrew."

He stood up and grabbed his coat off the other barstool. As he did, Candace reached out and touched the sleeve of his sweater, one he seemed to wear too often, and pulled her hand back as quickly. She stared at his face, as if seeing him for the first time. "It's cashmere."

"So I'm told." Amanda had been crazy about it, telling him he'd finally made it to the Style Channel.

Candace drew her brows together. "Mac, we *need* to talk."

He picked up his keys from the bar. "Another time. I have to get going." Amanda would be home soon, and he still needed to stop by Ellen's grave. The bar was across town from his house, distant enough that he had his privacy. Now that privacy was gone. Candace had known his story the whole time, and had her own to tell, one he didn't want to hear. The weight of everything pressed hard against him. He stepped away from the barstool, seeing the door as his goal.

"Merry Christmas, Mac," he heard from behind him.

When he looked back at her, he saw something he never expected. Tears. He turned away and darted for the door.

Chapter Thirty-Two

Amanda

Her dad was in a total funk. He had started feeding them frozen dinners, and last night he suggested they go to Rico's for a Stromboli, until he remembered that he had banned them from Rico's for life. Amanda thought her mom would want them to go back to Rico's and enjoy it again as they all had together, but he withdrew the offer, opting for a take-out pizza. Amanda made them a salad, continuing the healthy balance Sandy had started for them. They needed Sandy to ground them, to put her Mom's loss into perspective, and, mostly, to make them happy.

Amanda had a plan. She'd worked it out, at least in her mind. The plan was risky and might secure a spot on the Naughty List, but these were desperate times.

Unfortunately, Sandy was being even less cooperative than her dad. She had cancelled their after-school get-together—saying holiday sales were keeping her busy. Amanda assumed Sandy was stretching the truth to give herself more "time," so Amanda didn't feel too bad in coming up with a couple of "truth stretches" of her own. If these two supposed adults couldn't figure out how to get back together, Amanda would have to do it for them. The first little non-truth was telling Lacey's mom that Sandy was expecting her at Ginger's, but as she pulled up to the curb in front, Amanda immediately saw a potential kink.

Sandy was standing outside, arms wrapped around her ruffled coat, talking to Virgie. Sandy looked cold—and tense. Virgie, in her red, full-length coat and matching hat with a printed scarf, looked snuggly warm—and calm. Now that she thought about it, Virgie might be good to have on her side. Amanda thanked Lacey's Mom and jumped out of the car.

"Amanda, how lovely," Virgie said.

The tension on Sandy's face seemed to intensify, but she managed a smile.

"I hope you don't mind," Amanda said. "Mrs. Hoffman had an appointment and didn't have time to take me home." *Amanda McAllister—Naughty List.* "Dad's going to pick me up."

"He's coming *here*?" Sandy wrapped her arms tighter around her coat. "When?"

"Soon." Amanda couldn't commit to a time since she hadn't told him yet that she needed a ride.

"Why don't I take Amanda to Gourmet Delights?" Virgie offered. "We can have something warm to drink, and you can join us when you finish the tasks that have been keeping you so *busy*." Amanda knew a jab when she heard one. Sandy must have been giving her the same story. Virgie wasn't buying it either.

"I don't think . . ." Sandy closed her mouth and bit her lip. "I'll be there shortly." She huffed back into the store.

"We've ruffled her feathers," Virgie said.

"Now they match her coat." Amanda replied.

Virgie laughed. "Indeed. And it's a good thing. Let's go." She dashed away in her black pumps with chunky heels. Amanda thought they might take it slowly given Virgie's age, but she was glad to be wearing her low-heeled ankle boots—an early Christmas present she had convinced her dad she needed—to keep the pace.

They hoofed a block to Gourmet Delights, a small shop with an assortment of irresistible desserts. Amanda didn't attempt to resist. She pointed to a cinnamon twist while Virgie chose a less sinful piece of shortbread. Amanda wanted hot chocolate with marshmallows to complete the sugar fest, but Virgie ordered herbal tea with honey for them both. They settled into a table by the window, one with chairs with backs made of metal shaped into hearts. They weren't the most comfortable, but the design was definitely fitting for her task.

"Now," Virgie said, "did Mrs. Hoffman really have an appointment?"

Amanda took a sip of her tea. It did taste better than the water and tea bags she heated in the microwave at home. Maybe it was the honey, or simply the company. "My dad and Sandy aren't speaking to each other right now," she offered as explanation.

"Yes, I know."

"I had to do something."

Virgie took the piece of shortbread, delicately broke it in half, and set it on her plate.

Just like Sandy, Amanda thought.

"I'm afraid I was attempting interference of my own," Virgie said, "without much success. Perhaps your tactics will have more merit. What time will your father be here?"

"As soon as I fib one more time and text him that Sandy's too busy to bring me home and ask him to come by and pick me up." Amanda waited in case Virgie thought the last "fib" might make her a serial liar.

Virgie nodded with hesitant approval.

Amanda sent the text, knowing her dad would complain, but he'd come to pick her up anyway. She sent a second text to Chip, who said his role in getting them back together would be icing on the cake. "The *wedding* cake," he joked. Amanda had no idea what crazy idea might have entered his brain, but she felt better with more people on the job.

Virgie took a dainty sip of tea. "We can't push them together if they don't want to go, but I applaud your efforts."

"But what's coming between them?" Amanda asked. "Can't they just figure it out?"

"They can and they will, but it doesn't mean they'll figure it out the way we want. It has to be their decision. Our interfering won't help."

"I don't get it. He's miserable, but he won't call her. She looks miserable, too. Isn't it okay to interfere if it's with people you love?"

Virgie patted her hand, which Amanda took as another nod of approval. "We can try to set things in motion, but they must decide where that motion takes them."

"What if it doesn't take them anywhere? How can I go away to college if Dad is all by himself?"

"Yes, that does present a problem." Virgie broke off a small piece of the shortbread and put it in her mouth, chewing slowly. Amanda could almost see her thoughts turning over. "We do have a couple of years before you go to college to come up with a solution, but I don't think it will take that long."

Amanda's phone delivered her dad's response. "He's on his way." She paused. "I didn't tell him that you were here or that Sandy would be showing up."

"Well, then, won't it be a nice surprise for him?"

As surprises went, Amanda didn't see this one falling into the *Nice* category.

Ten minutes later, his truck pulled up outside. He waved to her, indicating he wouldn't be coming in. Amanda hurried outside, opened the passenger door, and stuck her head in. "Can you come in for minute? Virgie wants to meet you."

"Virgie? Sandy's grandmother?" He tightened his jaw. "Can't we do this another time?"

"Sure, if we want to be completely rude. She's nice, Dad, and she really wants to meet you."

He rubbed his chin, and she knew he wished he had shaved. He turned off the engine. "We're having a conversation later."

"Dad, we have conversations *all the time*. Last time we talked, I told you to call Sandy, remember?"

"I don't think it's a conversation when you're telling me what to do."

"Why not? You call it a conversation when you tell *me* what to do."

"That's why you call me 'Dad.'"

He rounded his truck and held open the door to Gourmet Delights for Amanda. Once they were inside, Virgie waved. He went to her and shook her hand. "I'm Bill McAllister."

"I'm Virginia Morgan. Thank you for coming to pick up Amanda. She's such a dear girl. Please join us. Would you like some tea?"

He sat in one of the chairs, leaned back and winced. "No, thank you. We can't stay long. I'm sure Amanda has homework." He leveled a warning glance at Amanda, which could either have been for the awkward situation she had put him in, or as a response to the uncomfortable chair.

"Amanda told me about your Christmas display," Virgie said. "Doesn't dressing up the house make the holidays so much more festive?"

He looked skeptical, as if it was a trick question, but Virgie's charm was hard to resist. "I've always thought so."

"I understand you're interested in older homes," Virgie said, continuing her quest to win him over. "They don't come much older than mine. You should come by to see it sometime. We've just finished with the holiday decorations. Sandy usually helps me, but she's been quite *busy*." She allowed the words to rest. Amanda guessed she wanted her dad to know he wasn't the only one Sandy had been avoiding. Virgie continued. "Some years I think I don't need a tree, and I don't, but the house does. The house was made to celebrate Christmas."

"A house doesn't celebrate Christmas," Amanda said.

"This one does," she countered. "The occupants come and go, but the house carries the tradition. The house thrives on love and was built for families to share." She waited a couple of beats before going back in to seal the deal. "Maybe you can come for dinner, when Sandy is more *available*." For all of her talk of a non-interference policy, Virgie seemed to be sticking her nose right in. Amanda was starting to love her.

Her dad caught Amanda's eye and held it. "We'll see." She waited for him to say it was time to go, but an approaching customer distracted him.

Sandy stopped when she saw him through the window, pushing her hair away from her face with her mitten and holding the length of it in the wind.

Amanda nudged him. "Open the door, Dad."

For once, he did what she told him. Sandy turned to look behind her, before she took a hesitant step forward, and another, finally making it to the door where he was waiting. After a polite exchange of, "Thank you," and an equally polite, "You're welcome," he closed the door behind her. Then they just stood there, looking at each other. "You look . . ." He couldn't seem to come up with a word.

Beautiful, Amanda thought. *Say beautiful, Dad.*

He continued to stare at her as if he couldn't decide how she looked. Amanda noticed Sandy had dark circle under her eyes, like her dad. They were so much alike. Now if they could just figure it out.

"*Nice,*" he finally said. "You look nice."

Amanda could only shake her head. Even Chip knew "nice" wasn't much of a compliment.

"I could have brought Amanda home," Sandy said. "You didn't need to make a special trip."

"According to a text I received from my daughter, I *did* need to make a special trip." They turned in unison toward Amanda who wished she could be smaller.

"If I didn't know better," he said, "I'd say we'd been set up. But I'm sure no one would ever do anything sneaky like that."

Sandy smiled. "A set-up? Oh no, not *our* Amanda."

Our. The word seemed to hang there, everyone aware of it. And it fit. She belonged to them, and they belonged to her.

"I've invited Amanda and her father to come by and see the house while it's decorated for Christmas," Virgie said.

Sandy laughed. "Well, Bill, you may as well bring your hammer and tool belt. She'll send you home for them anyway."

"So I'm invited?"

Three sets of eyes focused on Sandy, waiting for her answer, when a fourth set walked in the door. Chip had arrived, and he was wearing his marching band tuba over his shoulder. His older brother followed behind him, immediately sitting at the counter, pointing at the brownies and then the chocolate éclairs. Chip attempted to pull a chair up to the table but started to fall backward with the weight of the tuba. He leaned forward and pulled the tuba over his head, holding it out to her dad.

"Hey, Mr. M. Would you mind?"

Her dad scrunched his face as he always did when Chip was around, but took the instrument while Chip pulled up a chair and sat down as if he hadn't just walked in wearing a tuba.

"Thanks, Mr. M." He turned to Sandy. "He likes it when I call him that."

"I do?" her dad said.

"It was unspoken. Hey, Amanda."

"Hey, Chip. This is Mrs. Morgan, Sandy's grandmother."

"Oh my goodness," Virgie said. "We're back to formal. Next you'll be calling me 'ma'am' again." She held out her hand to Chip. "Call me Virgie. And I *do* like that name."

He shook her hand. "Hey, Virgie. I'm Charles Dugan Jr., Chip for short, and the human donut chute over there is my brother, Matt."

They all looked at Matt who was shoving a second brownie into his mouth.

"Pay the lady, Chip," Matt said, not bothering to cover his mouth. "Taxi services aren't free."

"Pardon me while I take care of another one of my malnourished taxi driver's tabs. I think it would be cheaper to take an actual taxi. When I turn sixteen, *I'll* be doing the driving." He winked at Amanda.

Her dad closed his eyes and Amanda could read his mind.

Chip paid the tab and returned to the table, relieving her dad of the tuba. "Now," he said, addressing her dad and Sandy, "Amanda tells me you have been a little down in the dumps, not your usual happy Christmas selves."

Her dad shot Amanda a glare that said they would *definitely* be having that talk later on.

"So I'm here to cheer you up," Chip said. "Cheering up is my specialty. Any requests?" He glanced at each one of them.

"You're going to play that thing?" her dad asked.

"Sure. That's why I'm here." He glanced at each one of them again, appearing confident that he could handle any request. As far as Amanda knew, he was limited to the National Anthem, the school fight song, some John Philip Sousa marches, and "Sweet Caroline." She was prepared to suggest it if no one had any other requests.

"Do you know any Christmas songs?" Sandy asked.

He took a big breath and put his lips on the mouthpiece. A low sound came out of the bell, then a second. He smiled. "Just warming up." He took another breath and began playing a song. After a few measures, Amanda recognized the song as some version of "Jingle Bells." She thought about helping out by singing along, but Chip seemed to be handling it fine on his own.

When he finished, he sat back. Virgie was the first to clap, followed by Sandy, then Amanda and finally her dad.

"Do you feel better?" Chip asked.

"I do," Virgie said. "I have much more holiday spirit now. I'm planning my annual Christmas Eve party. It's early in the evening, so everyone can be with their families later on. You're invited, Chip, and your family, and your tuba. Sandy will be there, and I was just getting around to inviting Bill and Amanda. You should all come. Matt," she called, "there will be prime rib and every kind of dessert possible."

"I'm in!" he replied, taking the last bite of his éclair.

"Me too," Chip said, "I mean if Amanda is going to be there."

Amanda put on her best hopeful face. "Will I be there, Dad?"

"It's up to Sandy."

"Of course," she said quickly. "You too, Bill." She folded her arms.

Amanda smiled at Chip, who was taking a breath to start a new song. She tugged on his jacket. "Why don't you surprise us on Christmas Eve? You know how Dad likes surprises."

Chip looked from Amanda to her dad to Sandy. "Oh. Okay. We're all cheered up then. I guess I'll save my finale." He pushed the tuba over his head and set it on the floor. "Nice to meet you, Virgie." He nodded. "Sandy." He nodded again. "Mr. M." He stood up. "See you in school, Amanda. Come on, taxi driver. You should be refueled by now."

"Hey, I could use some gas for the car," Matt said.

"Forget it. I know Mom told you that you *had* to drive me wherever I needed to go as part of your allowance. But nice try."

As Chip, Matt and the tuba walked out the door, Virgie said, "I'll need to order some more prime rib," Virgie said.

"And more desserts," Sandy said.

"And some aspirin," her dad added.

Virgie and Amanda laughed, but Sandy and her dad shared a glance and they both looked anxious. Amanda wondered if Christmas Eve would be a celebration. She could only shake her head—again. These two were making her job difficult, but she was aiming for an out-of-state college, and she was going to get there.

Chapter Thirty-Three

Bill

When he opened his front door and saw his father-in-law standing on his porch, Bill knew it was not a social visit. Visits from Andrew Waters were never social. Bill couldn't recall the last time Andrew had been at his doorstep. He assumed he had been in his house after Ellen's funeral, but the day was a blur of faces and condolences. The only clear image, besides holding onto Amanda at the cemetery as she cried, was someone handing him a piece of chocolate cake, as if the sugar in the gooey frosting might dull the reality he was struggling to accept. Maybe Andrew had a piece of that cake too. Bill didn't know. He didn't care.

"Is Lily with you?" Bill asked.

"No. She's moved into her condo. I need to talk to you alone."

Bill couldn't think of anything he wanted to do less than have a one-on-one conversation with his father-in-law. "Amanda's here."

"I'd like to see her, but maybe we can go out somewhere and talk."

At a time when he just wanted to shut his bedroom door and wait until Sandy was ready to have the conversation that would determine their future, everyone wanted to talk to him. He had to assume Candace's revelation and Andrew's appearance were connected. He could have lived without that story forever.

"May I come in?" Andrew asked.

Bill realized he'd been subconsciously blocking the door. He stepped aside and Andrew entered, filling the space in the small living room.

Amanda poked her head around the corner. "Grandpa?" She was beyond the age of giggling and running into her grandfather's arms. Like Bill, her immediate reaction was suspicion for the man who was out of place. She recovered quickly and stepped toward him for a hug. "I wished I knew you were coming. I just made plans with Lacey and Kate to go to Coffee Haven to study. We have a test tomorrow, but I can call and cancel."

"No, no. Tests are important, and I'll see you for Christmas." Andrew glanced at Bill. "I will, won't I, Mac?"

He nodded. He and Lily would see Amanda, but he was planning to drop her off and go some place—any place—else. One torturous holiday dinner per year with his in-laws was more than enough for him. This one promised to the worse than the last because the plan was to have dinner at Andrew's house, which was now being staged for sale, followed by dessert at Lily's new condo. Both scenes turned his stomach.

"I can take you to Coffee Haven," Bill offered, searching for an excuse to deflect the conversation.

"Lacey's mom is picking me up. Just think, Dad, next year, I'll be driving."

He groaned, first because he had no escape from Andrew and, second because Amanda refused to stop growing up. A horn sounded outside. "That's for me." Amanda said. "Everything's okay, isn't it, Grandpa?"

"Everything's fine."

Amanda eyed him warily.

Now that Bill had a chance to observe Andrew, he did appear a little ragged. Sleep seemed to have taken a holiday, which Bill knew too well.

Andrew straightened his shoulders, adding an inch to his height and a layer of cheeriness that came out as a forced smile. "I just came for a visit."

Amanda wasn't buying it. Bill liked that she knew BS when she heard it. If she had more time, he imagined the series of questions she would have asked, but she ran to her room and was back a minute later, backpack in hand. With a hug for Andrew and a kiss for Bill, she was gone.

Andrew waited until the door clicked before he delivered the line Bill knew was coming. "Does she always make plans without informing you?"

Bill could have said she was fifteen and she was studying with friends, but for once, he wasn't the one who needed to be on the defense. "Want a drink, Andrew? I'm having one."

"I'm driving." He rubbed his forehead, and the action seemed to deflate him. "Oh, hell. Give me a scotch." He threw his coat over the back of the couch and settled into Bill's favorite chair.

Bill accepted that his uninvited houseguest was here to stay, so he poured their drinks, scotch for Andrew and bourbon on the rocks for himself. Normally, he would have diluted his with Coke, but tonight called for a straight shot. He handed Andrew his drink, fell into a spot on the couch, and waited.

Andrew took a slow slip. "Do you have a coaster?"

Bill thought of the glass coasters Sandy had purchased for him, ones he had slid into a drawer when she started having doubts about their relationship. If she had been there, she would already have a coaster under Andrew's glass and she'd be serving him gourmet cheeses and tiny crackers on a fancy plate. She'd make him feel welcome, but "welcome" was not something Bill wanted to say to Andrew Waters. "We're informal here."

Andrew took another sip and exhaled. Only then did he venture a glance at Bill. "You know that I never thought you were good enough for Ellen. I always thought she should marry a professional—an attorney, doctor, some corporate executive—someone who didn't wear work boots." He drained the last drop from his glass and set it on the end table. "Probably none of them would have been good enough for her either."

Bill glanced at Andrew's polished black shoes, probably some designer brand that Sandy would recognize. The shoes looked tight and uncomfortable. All those years, he wanted Andrew's approval, but he was never going to fit into the shoes Andrew had hoped for his daughter. He didn't have to try anymore.

"I was angry with you," Andrew said, "but then again, I'd been angry for a long time, mostly at myself. It was easy to take some of that anger out on you, particularly after Ellen's death. If you'd still been living in Lafayette, she wouldn't have been on that road that night. I wanted to blame someone, but it was a horrible accident and it was no one's fault." He picked up his drink as if he'd forgotten it was empty. He set it back down.

Bill was amazingly unaffected by Andrew's words. "You drove for two hours to tell me things I already know?"

"No. I drove for two hours to tell you I'm an ass. I suppose you already know that too. You should also know that I'm a hypocrite. Is the scotch in the kitchen?"

"On the counter."

Andrew grabbed his glass. He returned with more scotch, although he'd added ice. "I can get a hotel room."

Bill could have offered the guest room, but Andrew in a hotel sounded fine to him.

Andrew took a drink and gripped the armrest of the chair with his other hand. "Candace called me."

Bill had hoped he'd been able to evade hearing about Candace's relationship with Andrew, but the story had come to door. He had no idea why he was suddenly his father-in-law's confessor.

"If you're going to continue," Bill said, "I'm going to need another drink."

By the time he reached the kitchen, Bill had changed his mind. He wanted to be alert for the saga Andrew seemed intent on telling him. He added more ice and filled his glass with Coke. He returned to the living room. "Okay," he said. "Let's hear it."

Andrew straightened his posture. "I was in my twenties. Without outlining the difficulties Lily and I were having at the time, other than we were separated when I met Candace, I'll just say Candace and I had an affair."

"I assumed the story was going in that direction."

"Yes, but you need to also know that Candace and I had a daughter."

Bill thought he was ready for any sordid detail Andrew felt compelled to share, but not for this announcement. "What do you want me to say—Congratulations? Why are telling me this?"

He took a drink, wishing he'd gone for the bourbon. When Andrew remained silent, Bill filled in his own explanation. "Don't tell me you want Amanda to meet her." He was already imagining the scene. It would be awkward as hell.

"Amanda already has met her. In fact," he said carefully, "I understand they're quite close."

Bill tried to imagine someone Amanda knew who could be Andrew's daughter. A teacher, perhaps? A neighbor? He shook his head.

"Sandy," Andrew said. "Candace and I didn't know you were seeing one another."

Bill fought to put the pieces together. Sandy rarely talked about her mother. She may have mentioned her by name; he didn't recall. Sandy said she'd met her father—her *real* father. He couldn't quite grasp it. The man sitting in front of him seemed nothing like the father Bill had imagined for her or, likely, the one she had imagined for herself. The thought of Sandy being disappointed and hurt by this man, who'd already spent years rejecting Bill, ignited his fury.

"Sandy is your daughter? Your *daughter?*" All the doubt, the fear of losing Sandy, the loneliness, every emotion simmering inside him turned to anger. "*You're* the deadbeat she's been looking for?"

Andrew glued his eyes to ice cubes in his empty glass. "I'm the deadbeat."

Sandy's actions of the last few weeks fell into place, and her words pierced him. *If your feelings come from a place of wanting what you had—of filling the loss—it won't be enough to sustain us.* He understood why she had needed some time.

"I'm not going to try to defend my actions," Andrew said. "I'll only say that I loved Ellen. I didn't want to be separated from her, which would have happened if I chose Candace and Sandy. I was also ambitious, and working with my father-in-law's firm allowed me the position I wanted. I made a decision and I have to live with it."

232

"You mean *Sandy* has to live with it. And now Amanda and I have to live with it." He ran his hand through his hair. "God, Andrew, what am I going to tell Amanda?"

"I don't know. If you and Sandy care about each other, you can work it out. I wasted years thinking Ellen should have a different life when she was happy every day with you. You deserve a chance to be happy again and so does Sandy. Talk to her. I don't know what she's thinking."

"I don't know what I'm thinking either." Bill stood up. "I need to get out of here. You can wait for Amanda, but *don't say anything*!" He grabbed his coat from the closet and slammed the door.

He stormed past the snow village, the scene now taunting him with its happiness. He leveled a scowl at Andrew's Mercedes parked on the street, knowing the man had paid a high price for his success. He jumped into his truck and threw it into reverse, forcing himself to take a breath and pull out of his driveway slowly as he noticed a car driving past to view the display. People were still celebrating the season, even if the joy had left his world.

He drove without knowing a destination, ending up on Main Street, Christmas displayed in full wattage. Lights and garland streamed from wreathed lamppost to lamppost with Santa and his reindeer in the center median. It felt like a movie set now, offering the impression of a happy scene, but acting only as a front for the emptiness behind it.

He slowed when he drove by Althea's, the flickering lights beckoning him and repelling him at the same time. A few minutes later, he was outside Sandy's house. He parked, but left the engine running. The light was on in the living room with her Christmas tree twinkling in the window. All he had to do was knock on the door. In a minute, he could be holding her, telling her it was okay.

It started to rain, reminding him of that first night when he kissed her under his umbrella. He could almost feel her in his arms, but he still couldn't force himself out of his truck. He needed time to think, to process, just as she had needed time. Right now, the weight was too heavy for him to carry.

The curtain fluttered and Sandy peered out the window. She may have seen him, but the thought of looking into her brown eyes and touching her silky hair sent another wave of doubt through him. He put the gearshift into drive.

Bill circled Main Street again, turning the opposite direction from home. He passed The Rusty Nail and almost laughed. If he went in and Candace was working, family night would be complete. He pulled into the cemetery as the rain turned to sleet.

He parked in the familiar spot, pulled up the hood on his coat and grabbed a flashlight from the glove compartment. He'd become accustomed to wandering the path at night. Sometimes the moon would light the way, but there was no moonlight tonight.

A few minutes later, he was standing at Ellen's headstone. He read the words that he had read a hundred times. *Ellen Waters McAllister. Wife. Mother. Daughter.* Now they could add *Sister* to the list.

Ellen would have loved to have a sister. She always wondered if she had siblings somewhere, but she'd never wanted to hurt her parents by pursuing her biological family. How ironic. She'd been so selfless when her parents had been selfishly hiding an important truth.

"I don't know what to do, Ellen. I guess I could let it go. I could pretend Sandy never happened, as your father did. Maybe knowing the truth would always be between Sandy and me. Maybe *you* would always be between us. Except . . ." Bill wiped his face with his sleeve, and looked up toward the sky, "you weren't that kind of person. She's not that kind of person. You said we should always choose happiness."

The sleet was heavier now. He closed his eyes, remembering the way Ellen always had the right words to soothe his bad moods. "I'm so grateful for the life we had together, and for Amanda. Maybe it's enough. Maybe a person's only allowed so much happiness. God knows, you gave me more than my share."

As he turned to leave, his flashlight swept across Ellen's grave. Someone had laid a new wreath. His first thought was Andrew, who might have stopped by before he came to the house. He knelt down to study the wreath, which was made of pine branches with small brown cones and a large red bow. Attached to the needles were a dozen ornaments.

All Santas.

Tears stung his eyes. "Oh, Ellen. She loves you, too."

Chapter Thirty-Four

Candace was hiding in the stock room, taking inventory when she should have been waiting on customers. Hank, her business partner of fifteen years, had told her to take the night off. She hated the thought of waiting at home for a call from Andrew. She glanced at her watch. Nine o'clock. Enough time for Andrew to have seen Mac and told him Sandy's identity. Enough time for him to phone Candace and tell her about Mac's reaction. Certainly enough time for him to think that she might be waiting and wondering if their daughter was about to have her heart broken in a way that couldn't be fixed.

Hank opened the door, holding her coat. "You're useless to me tonight." He wore his favorite blue work shirt. His hair was white now reminding her that the plan had been for him to retire and for her to take over the bar. She paused. Had it really been fifteen years? She'd bought into the business with some help from Art who told her she needed something with a future. A bar wasn't something she ever thought she needed, or wanted, but Hank made the workload bearable. They needed each other. Their partnership meant Hank had more evenings at home with his wife and Candace had a way to support herself in a place she enjoyed. It all worked, until recently when she'd started thinking of a different life.

Talking to Andrew, if only over the phone, had started her down this path again.

She'd never planned to stay this long in St. Clair. Days had turned into weeks, weeks into months, and with barely a blink, years had slipped away. The plans she'd made when she was young had bubbled up, reminding her of the life she had desired outside of her home town.

"You're over thinking again," Hank said.

"It's Andrew. Talking to him again has me questioning everything. Why does he have this effect on me?"

"We all have our weak spots. Give him a call. You don't have to wait on him anymore." He knew her story and had encouraged her over the years to have faith that she had made the right decisions.

"You're right. I don't. Old habit, I guess. Thanks." She set down the inventory list that was still nearly blank and took her coat.

The bar was filling up with customers, the buzz starting for the band on the schedule for nine-thirty. Rachel, the other bartender Hank had called in to cover Candace's shift, was serving up beers and mock flirting with some of the regulars. With her braids, tight jeans and cowboy boots, she did well in the tip department. Hank knew how to hire the right employees. He'd managed for years before Candace arrived. The last few months, she'd been imagining Hank without her again and herself in a different place. They hadn't had that conversation yet, but Hank knew her well. He likely suspected it was coming.

Candace felt a dose of guilt, and almost hung up her coat, until she looked toward the door and he came into view. His temples had grayed and the creases around his eyes had deepened. Andrew took a few steps toward her and stopped, filling the space she didn't know had been empty.

He'd been in the bar twice before.

Before the accident, he had come to tell her that Ellen was moving to St. Clair. They took as a sign that it was time to tell the truth, and for them to have a second chance. They had talked about moving to a new place where Andrew could start his own law practice and live without the scrutiny of his father-in-law. She would find a job in a small restaurant, one without the late hours of a bar. They could still be close to Ellen and Sandy, but far enough away to allow them their own lives. The dream almost became a reality—until the worst possible thing in the world happened.

The second time he walked through that door was a month after Ellen's funeral. On that day, he wore a steel grey pin-stripe suit, a heavily starched white shirt with a narrow collar and a dark blue tie with tiny red arrows—funny how she remembered every detail. He wore the stiff clothes like armor, delivering the news that he was going back to Lily. As much as she wanted to blame Lily for pulling him back to her, Andrew had made the choice. A layer of guilt seemed to compel him to stay, as if Ellen's death meant they no longer deserved their chance at happiness. At a time when Candace felt he needed her most, he had closed her off. He thought he was releasing her to go on with her life without him, but he didn't have that power.

Tonight he wore a jacket, but he'd cast his tie aside. He looked similar to the first time she saw him when he'd walked into the coffee house. He was professional, but approachable, with an air of confidence that drew her toward him like a powerful magnet. After thirty years, she should have developed some immunity to him. It had never happened.

"I'm sorry I'm late," he said. "Mac left the house, and I waited for Amanda to come home from studying. I thought I'd stay there until Mac got back, but apparently, Amanda is going to college 'soon,' and is perfectly capable of staying in the house alone."

"I thought you would call."

"I wanted to see you." He took a moment to observe her. "You always did like boots."

She had to admit, she had a collection. Her black riding boots worn over jeans were this season's favorites. He always noticed how she looked, and compliments usually followed. She didn't need compliments tonight. "How did it go with Mac?"

"I'm definitely off his Christmas list, but he was very defensive of Sandy. I think it's a good sign." He surveyed the bar, his eyes landing on the band that was finishing their sound check. "Can we go somewhere?"

"We are somewhere."

He glanced around for a place to sit. Patrons had filled the booths and the tables. He gestured to the two spaces still available at the bar.

He sat down and she slid onto the barstool next to him. Hank was already pouring them each a shot of Jameson. Not many customers ordered the expensive whiskey. She and Hank kept it mainly for themselves. He set the shots in front of them, adding a glass of Coke for Candace, and nodded with encouragement. She felt a surge of gratitude for her good friend.

Andrew eyed the shot warily. "I'm definitely going to need a hotel room tonight." He took a sip, set down the glass, and reached over for a drink of her coke. The action reminded her of the moments they had as a couple when sharing a drink—or a hamburger—was completely natural. He finished his whiskey and pushed the glass away. "I saw Sandy today."

"What did she say?"

"I didn't talk to her. I think she has some things to work out with Mac before I attempt to have a conversation with her. I just saw her outside her store. She walked out the front door wrapped in some scarf when she should have been wearing a coat."

"It's Pashmina. Sandy believes in fashion at the expense of comfort."

"She's independent. Like you."

"She's not like me." Sandy was more like him than he might ever know. She was precise, organized and annoyingly inflexible.

"She has your brown eyes and your petite frame and she doesn't let anyone intimidate her."

"How would you know?"

"She's our daughter. She's strong and confident. I knew it when she walked into my office. We've tried too hard to protect her and ended up hurting her more. Let's stop. She and Mac will work it out or they won't. I do believe, however, that if they had known each other when Ellen was alive, they may not have had this opportunity. We made the best decisions we could. It's time to let it go."

Candace considered his words, while she focused her attention on the string of lights that had drooped at the top of the bar. It had been that way for days. Sandy would have fixed it immediately, unable to suppress her need for order. Sandy was like him, but she had Candace in her too. He was right. Sandy didn't need her to protect her anymore. It was time to let her go.

"And it's also time for Lily and me to get a divorce," he said. "Being together has never really lessened the pain of losing Ellen. Now it's just a matter of the paperwork."

"I'm sorry, Andrew." She didn't know what else to say, and he didn't seem to be looking for anything. Luckily, the band started playing, making it impossible to have meaningful conversation. They'd probably had too many meaningful conversations over the years anyway. She'd almost forgotten that when they first met, they'd actually had fun.

The band had changed their usual set. They typically started with an upbeat song to get the crowd on the dance floor, but tonight, they began with a slower Keith Urban song. Couples filtered out onto the floor. Andrew put his hand over hers. "Let's dance."

She took a moment to enjoy his touch. "We've never danced together." When they began seeing one another, she was too young to go to bars. It felt like another lifetime.

"Then it must be time." He led her to the floor and his arms folded around her. Candace put her head on his shoulder and they swayed gently to the music. She had no idea where they would go from here, or even if they could. She only knew that, in that moment, she felt happy and content to be with him.

Tomorrow would take care of itself.

Chapter Thirty-Five

Sandy

Sandy opened her front door, expecting to see Candace, or Virgie, maybe Amanda or possibly Bill. The last person she expected to see was Trent.

"Hey, Sandy," he said casually, hunching his shoulders as he often did. Sandy scrutinized the plaid in his heavy wool jacket, a large pattern of muted terra cotta and turquoise, imagining it as a shirt in a smaller pattern with Bill wearing it, which would mean he was standing at her door.

She still hadn't found the courage to contact Bill, but she'd been practicing their conversation. She'd explain the unbelievable circumstances to the best of her knowledge and let him decide what path their lives might take. He would have to choose if he wanted to tell Amanda about her. It didn't seem fair to him to put the responsibility of the decision on him, but nothing about the situation was fair. She'd also tell him that whatever his reaction, she'd hoped they could at least still be friends. *Friends.* She hated even thinking the word, but it might be all they could have.

However, right now, she didn't have to fight that emotional battle because Trent was still standing at the door. "In the neighborhood?" she asked.

"I wanted to bring you this." He held out a small poinsettia plant, which, until he called her attention to it, had been invisible. To his credit, it appeared he had remembered she preferred the smaller plants rather than the oversized ones, or perhaps it was only a price-based decision driven by a cost-benefit analysis—the cost of the plant vs. the likelihood Sandy would let him in the door.

"How's Francesca?"

He drew back. "Good, I suppose. I mean I still see her at work, but we're not . . ."

"Oh." Sure. Why not visit your old girlfriend when things have gone south with the new one? "She seemed . . ." How had she seemed? Sandy could barely remember her. "She seemed nice."

"Can I come in?"

Sandy held back her desire to correct his grammar, at least for a few seconds. "Yes, you *may* come in."

Inside, she didn't know quite what to do with him. He shuffled awkwardly while she occupied herself by mentally grabbing a pair of scissors and cutting his hair. The professional cut was gone, replaced by the longer hair she had always liked but now seemed shabby. Perhaps he was telling her that he was his old self again—the one she knew. He was here with some sort of peace offering. Should she adhere to the manners Virgie taught her and offer him a seat, followed by a choice of beverages?

Trent made the choice for her by handing her the plant and seating himself on the couch. She set the small plant next to the burlap-coated Santa on the mantel. It was an unfair comparison, but placing the gifts side-by-side made the differences even more pronounced. She turned back to her uninvited guest. "Wine?"

"That'd be great."

Virgie would be proud of her manners. Sandy didn't know what she was feeling.

In the kitchen, she removed an open bottle of Chardonnay from the fridge. She poured half a glass, deciding half a glass should give him time to say whatever it was he came to say. She refrained from pouring herself a glass, which would have made the scene a little too cozy.

Trent had removed his coat, revealing a heavy cotton sweater Sandy had given him for Christmas last year. She categorized the appearance of the sweater as another sign of contrition. She didn't want him to be contrite. She didn't want him to be anything. She handed him the glass of wine. He took a drink, and a second. He placed the glass on the coaster as she always asked, but he rarely did.

"How is it?" she asked.

"It's good. Isn't it from the case we bought last summer? Remember that trip?" He took her hand, and she wished she opened a new bottle of wine that didn't stir memories for him. His hand felt small and cold, the cold part not his fault given the temperature outside. But still.

He held her with expectant eyes, forcing her to remember that trip when they drank too much wine and fell into an antique four post-bed at an upstate B&B. He had been attentive—too attentive she could see now, so he was probably already cheating on her, if not in body, in spirit. And she had been doing the same thing to him. But she didn't feel guilty. Not anymore.

"It was a good trip, don't you think?" he asked. "I could make reservations at that B&B again. They're not busy in the winter."

And rates are better, Sandy thought. "So what happened with Frankie?"

He drew his hand back. "I didn't come to talk about Frankie. I came to talk about us."

"What 'us'? 'Us' is over."

"It's not over if you don't want it to be."

Leave it to Trent to know when she was vulnerable. "You're thinking about the past, when you should be thinking about the future."

"I *am* thinking about the future."

"Not the right one. We had our time, and I wouldn't change it, but it's over. Why are you here anyway? Did you and Frankie have a fight?"

Trent glanced at her Christmas trees laden with garland, ribbons and ornaments, shaking his head. She could almost read his mind. *Too much, Sandy. It's too much.* She waited for him to answer her question, but his hesitation had already given him away. "She doesn't understand me the way you did."

"You mean she doesn't indulge you the way I did."

"I indulged you, too," he retorted. He glanced at the trees again. She supposed it was number one on his list of indulgences.

"I agree, but I liked who you were, and the way we were together. It doesn't mean that another person, like Frankie, will accept the same behavior."

"It didn't seem like you liked me, at least not for the last few months we were together. It felt like you were trying to make me into a different person."

I was, she thought. Maybe she'd been unfair to him, but she wasn't going to start over with Trent. Even if Bill made the choice to end it with her, Trent was not going to be an option.

245

"Frankie may want a different kind of relationship with you. I don't know her. I do know that you and I have different futures. Now you need to go."

"Go? I just got here."

She could have reminded him that he was uninvited, but Virgie's manners prevailed. "Thank you for the present." She stood, ready to escort him out the door, but couldn't allow him to leave empty handed. She grabbed a bottle of wine accented with a bow from under the tree, a Napa Valley cabernet that she knew he liked. She pushed it toward him. "Merry Christmas."

He reluctantly accepted it. "Everyone gets a present, right?"

"Everyone gets a present." She opened the door and sent him grumbling out into the cold.

She watched through the window as he drove away, waiting for a twinge of melancholy. It didn't come. She was in love with someone else. He was across town surrounded by his beloved snowmen. She realized she hadn't seen the final outcome of Bill's creativity and hard work—his snow village. It couldn't hurt to just take a peek. She grabbed her keys and her coat and was out the door.

She headed toward the center of town, barely tapping the brake, defying any light that dared to turn yellow. Why the need to be there had suddenly turned urgent, she couldn't say, but she *needed* to get to Bill and Amanda. She approached Bill's street, turned on her blinker, and stopped behind a gridlock of cars. She offered a few rarely spoken swear words.

The traffic inched forward. As she neared the display, a parked car signaled the driver was vacating a coveted spot. She slammed on her brakes, and the car pulled out. She maneuvered into the spot, demonstrating a parking prowess she didn't know she possessed, and turned off the lights and engine. A magical wonderland sparkled in front of her.

Hills of fake snow showcased Bill's mechanical snowmen. One group of happy snow people repeatedly slid down a hill. Another group skated across a pond. Two snow children swayed back and forth on a swing attached to his large elm tree. A chorus of snow carolers appeared to belt out, "Winter Wonderland." The mischievous boy and the snowman target were freely exchanging snowballs, or tennis balls painted white. Bill's vision played at every corner.

A crowd milled in front, parents parking and walking to bring their children to live the experience firsthand. In the midst was a redhead she recognized as Gwen. Sandy's heart fell at the possibility that she was too late. A minute later, Gwen took the hand of a man Sandy didn't recognize and moved on.

Now there was no Gwen standing between them, and definitely no Trent. Only the truth remained as a barrier.

The crowd in front of the garage cleared. Amanda, dressed in an elf costume, was passing out Styrofoam cups to the kids. She was probably serving hot chocolate, Sandy's favorite. Bill stepped through the door, wearing a red fleece jacket and a Santa hat. He set down another tray of cups, which she assumed was coffee since he handed them out to the adults. Soon Amanda's cups were all gone, and she began filling new ones from a carafe.

Seeing both of them brought a smile, then a little pain in her heart. She needed to go.

Sandy pressed the ignition and started to put her car in drive when her cell phone rang. She grabbed the phone from her purse, surprised when it announced Bill as the caller. She looked toward the house and could see Bill with his pressed phone against his ear, but he wasn't looking in her direction.

"Bill?" she answered.

She could see him smiling. "Hey there. Listen, I know you were going to call when you're ready to talk, but I was wondering what you were doing this evening. Are you busy?"

"I'm a little busy, but I could make time."

His smile turned to a grin. "Great. I'm tied up here for another hour or so, but I could come over later, if that works."

"How about I come to your house?" she said.

"I don't want to make it difficult for you."

"How about I'm at your house right now?"

He scanned the crowd. "Where?"

She stepped out of the car and waved.

"I'll come to you," he said and hung up his phone.

She took a few steps toward the house and waited, as Bill weaved through the crowd frantic with Christmas spirit. They met on the sidewalk, stopping short of embracing.

"Hey," he said, grasping her hand. "I'm sorry I didn't call sooner, but I wanted to see you in person. I wanted to wait to talk to Amanda until after her volleyball tournament, and then we had to get set up for tonight."

Sandy's heart beat faster. "Talk to Amanda about what?"

"About you and Ellen." He looked puzzled. "Didn't Andrew tell you he came to see me?"

"*Andrew* came to see you? But you don't get along."

"We don't, and quite honestly, I wanted to punch the guy, but maybe I've wanted to do that for a long time. I figured I wouldn't be making a good impression on your father if I punched him."

"You know he's my father, and you talked to Amanda?"

He grinned. "I do, and I did."

"What did she say?"

"She said, 'I told you Mom would like Sandy.'"

They both turned in Amanda's direction. Chip had joined her, wearing elf ears. If he hadn't been passing out hot chocolate and coffee, Sandy thought he might break into a dance.

Bill turned back to Sandy. "You know you could have told me. What did you think I would do?"

"I didn't know. I suppose I wanted to hang on to you and Amanda just a little longer, in case it didn't work out. Are you sure?"

"Do you have any idea what it's been like for me not knowing what you're thinking or if you were coming back to me?"

She took a hard look at this man that she loved. The shadows under his eyes were less visible and he had a fresh shave. He'd been in a dark place, as she had, but they were both freeing themselves to begin again. "Yes, I think I do."

"Then you'll know I'm sure. I love you, Sandy." She'd been waiting to hear those words. "I want us to be together—the three of us."

The three of us. She liked the sound of it.

She felt something wet on her nose. Tiny snowflakes began to fall all around. She held out her hand, catching a few flakes and then closing her mittens to hold onto them.

He opened his arms and Sandy nestled into them. Moonlight broke through the clouds, highlighting the leafless maple in Bill's yard, flakes catching on the branches. She smiled at the beauty of the scene as she melted into him, his love protecting her from the cold. She had never felt so warm.

Chapter Thirty-Six

Amanda

Christmas Eve was Amanda's favorite day of the year. Holiday spirit was at its maximum, but they still had the anticipation of Christmas. Her dad always put off his shopping until Christmas Eve, and this year was no exception. Sandy may have been an overachiever in her early shopping, but she'd had no impact on his old habits.

He'd dropped Amanda off at Virgie's so she could help with the party prep, while he dashed around warming up his credit card. Virgie had hired caterers, but she managed to keep Amanda busy, mainly refining the decorations of her already beautifully decorated home. She especially loved the ten-foot artificial Christmas tree—with its vintage style blinking lights and pink, silver, and gold ornaments—that took up the whole picture window in the living room. Christmas music played in the background, along with the sound of the caterers clinking plates and glasses.

Amanda had taken up a sentry position next to the tree in a wingback chair that allowed her a view of the street and front walkway. She had already changed into her new black velvet holiday dress that had just the right amount of lace and sequins. With Sandy around, she'd never have to worry about finding the perfect item. Sandy made shopping an art.

She was happy that Sandy was around again. Sandy and her dad were already making plans for a future with each other, which included remodeling her house. When her dad showed the blueprints to Sandy, she'd asked him when he started working on the plans. He replied, "The day I met you." Sandy had blushed, and Amanda knew he got it right. They hadn't talked about moving in together yet—or at least they hadn't mentioned it to Amanda—but she knew it was coming. She wouldn't mind. The plans included a master suite on the first level, which meant Amanda could have some privacy upstairs. Not a bad life for a teenager, if she did say so herself. With the three of them plus all of the Santas and snowmen, the house was going to be full. Sandy said it was like love. There was always room for more.

The "more" might also include visits from her grandpa.

After her dad told her that Sandy was her grandpa's daughter, she found herself staring at Sandy looking for a resemblance. She couldn't see any physical characteristics, except maybe a little in the shape of their eyes, but she could see her grandpa in Sandy's obsession with tailored clothing. She didn't know if it was possible for such a trait to be hereditary, or just coincidence, but there it was. Her mom had been the opposite, wearing loose, baggy pants, long flowing skirts and oversized sweaters. She wondered what her mom's real parents had been like, if they had similar styles and habits. By now, her mom probably knew who they were. Amanda hoped she liked them.

She still wished her mom were here, so she could talk to her. Especially about Chip. In the last couple of months, he'd grown an inch or two. They were literally starting to see eye-to-eye. He said he'd be up to 6'5" soon and would snagging a spot on the Indiana Pacers.

Chip's tuba stood ready in the corner, set for the duet with Virgie on the piano. He'd come by earlier in the day and they'd practiced "Silent Night" and "Jingle Bells," deciding on "We Wish you a Merry Christmas" as their finale so everyone could sing along. Their version had a slight drag to it. The crowd would have to adjust its tempo.

The "crowd" would include Virgie's friends—too many names rattled off for Amanda to remember. Sandy had invited her employees and their significant others, and her dad had invited some of his co-workers at Virgie's encouragement. Virgie had also suggested Amanda invite as many friends as she wanted.

"Wouldn't it be the most boring party for you if you had to spend hours with us old folks?" Virgie had said. Lacey and her parents said they'd stop by after an early church service. Of course, Chip was bringing his whole family, including his parents, Matt (who'd been talking about prime rib for days) and Sam, Chip's little brother. Sam was also very excited and said he bet that Santa would leave one of his presents there. Amanda had checked, and there was a present under the tree with his name on it. She wasn't certain who had been the Santa, but the Man with the Bag had definitely been there.

She heard the sound of boots on the hard wood floor in the entryway and thought for a minute that he'd come back to deliver more presents. It was only Sandy's mom, who insisted Amanda call her Candace. It felt a little weird to call her by her first name, but that was apparently how they did things in her new family. Candace seemed to be slinking out the door.

"Are you leaving?" Amanda called.

Candace popped her head into the living room. She was still wearing her jeans and sweater with her hair pulled back into a ponytail. "Oh hello, Amanda. I didn't realize you were in here. I am leaving."

"But you'll be back." Sandy had gone home to change, so she assumed Candace was going to do the same.

"No. I won't be back. I've participated in enough eggnog toasts that Virgie's giving me a pass this year."

"We're having an eggnog toast?"

"Every year on Christmas Eve. We toast Jesus for his birthday. Personally, I think he'd prefer champagne, or maybe that's just me. You'll have a good time. My mother throws a good party. I am sorry to miss the tuba concert though." She winked. "Be sure to sing loud."

"Are you going to see Grandpa tonight?" Sandy had told her that Candace and her grandpa might spend time together, so Amanda wouldn't be surprised.

Candace entered the room and sat on the other wingback chair. "We're meeting for dinner. He said he's looking forward to seeing you tomorrow."

"Are you dating him?" It seemed weird to talk about her grandpa dating, but she guessed old people dated too. The last time she visited her grandma Lily, she seemed to be flirting with a man who lived in her condo complex. She did seem happier living alone. And she had a new puppy—too yappy for Amanda's taste, but her grandmother was in love.

"We're a little beyond dating," Candace said, "but I'll see him sometimes. I have some other plans right now." She glanced up the stairs. Virgie had gone up earlier to rest and then to get ready for the party. "Can you keep a secret?"

"I'm good at secrets," Amanda said.

She laughed. "I'm telling you my secret because I really want to get to know you, but right now I need some time away, to do things I've put off for too long. Hank, my partner, and I are selling our business to the other bartender, Rachel, and her husband. Hank's going to retire and I'm going to travel for a few months. I need some time on my own. I would like us to be friends, but I won't have much time to spend with you before I go."

"We can be friends," Amanda said. "I'm not going away to college for two years, so we'll have time."

She smiled, and Amanda could see Sandy in her. It was funny. Amanda wasn't related to Sandy, Virgie or Candace at all, but they already felt like family. Maybe it was because now Amanda knew they'd always been there, even if she hadn't known them.

"Did you know my mom?"

"When she was young, yes. She was a beautiful child, and very sweet."

"Can you tell me about her?"

"She loved being outside, like Sandy, but unlike Sandy, she hated wearing dresses. Dirt and mud were her friends. Her hair was baby fine. It would never stay in a ponytail. She liked running and jumping over anything in sight. I gave her a jump rope, and she would sing and jump at the same time. Your mom…" She paused for a minute. "Your mom was very special. I wish I'd had more time with her. I'm sorry for all the years she missed with Sandy and for the years Sandy missed with you."

"It's okay. She makes Dad happy, so I guess it worked out."

Candace smiled. "I guess it did." She turned back to Amanda. "You look beautiful, by the way. Chip is one lucky future NBA star."

"He jokes a lot."

"He was joking? Too bad. He said he'd let me ride in his limousine, you know, when he's famous. I figure if the whole basketball star thing doesn't work out, he has a promising music career." She winked again.

"How long should I keep your secret?"

"Probably until after New Year's. It's okay to have secrets sometimes. You just can't hold onto them forever." She stood up. "Have fun tonight, and Merry Christmas." She started toward the door.

"Are you my new grandma?" Amanda called.

"Bite your tongue." She laughed and was out the door.

Candace jumped into her sports car and drove away. A couple minutes later, her dad parked his truck in front and turned off the engine. When he got out, Amanda was happy to see he'd worn the clothing she had picked out for him—a sport coat over a new white dress shirt and a tie with a design that repeated, "Let it Snow," in red script. He came around the front of the truck and opened the door. Sandy stepped out wearing her ruffled coat and boots. Underneath her coat, Amanda saw a red dress peak out, which she assumed included some tribute to Santa. She and her dad would never agree on the topic of Santas vs. snowmen, but they joined hands and began to walk up the sidewalk together. They paused for a moment and laughed. He leaned over and gave her a quick kiss. Yep. People were never too old to date.

Chip's mom's van pulled up next, taking the spot behind her dad's truck. Sam darted out the door first, running through leftover snow from last week's storm to greet the lighted Santa and reindeer in the yard. His mom shouted to him while Chip and the rest of the family piled out. Chip was wearing his favorite oversized suit coat and he'd added a Christmas tie that he'd shown to Amanda with a picture of a snowman on it (to impress her dad), but he hadn't given up his black and white checkered Vans.

Another car parked behind them, and then another. *Punctual group*, Amanda thought.

She called up the stairs to Virgie and then went to open the door to greet the guests.

The party was about to begin.

Acknowledgements

Thank you to David, my wonderful husband, for encouraging my hobby and for the gift of a laptop all those years ago. I finally get to write "The End" to one of my stories, which would never have happened without you.

I am grateful to Diane Hull, my fellow Santa enthusiast, my editor, my friend. I'd love to know how many minutes we spent on the phone talking about the characters as if they were real people. You helped bring them to life and allowed them to live between the covers of this book. Here's to more projects together and more characters that keep us awake at night.

I appreciate the contributions of Caren Halvorsen for her beautiful cover art work and Vince Migliore for his work in formatting and helping to navigate the unfamiliar waters of self-publishing. I extend a special thank you to Karen Dale Harris for her guidance with ideas and editing suggestions to keep the story light and engaging.

Thank you to Mom who encouraged my love of reading, and to my funny, sweet, and brave sister, Janet Taylor, who also loved a good book.

And thank you to all of the readers out there who take the time to go on this journey. I hope you enjoy spending the holidays with Sandy, Bill and Amanda as much as I did.

Made in the
USA
Monee, IL